Dar and the Spear-Thrower

Dar and the Spear-Thrower

by Marjorie Cowley

CLARION BOOKS ▲ NEW YORK

Clarion Books
a Houghton Mifflin Company imprint
215 Park Avenue South, New York, NY 10003
Text copyright © 1994 by Marjorie Cowley
Illustration copyright © 1994 by Kate Kiesler

Text is 12-point New Baskerville

For information about this and other Houghton Mifflin
trade and reference books and multimedia products, visit
The Bookstore at Houghton Mifflin on the World Wide Web
at (http://www.hmco.com/trade/).

Printed in the USA

Library of Congress Cataloging-in-Publication Data

Cowley, Marjorie.
    Dar and the spear-thrower / by Marjorie Cowley.
        p.   cm.
    Summary: A young Cro-Magnon boy living 15,000 years ago
in southeastern France is initiated into manhood by his clan and
sets off on a journey to trade his valuable fire rocks for an ivory
spear-thrower.
        ISBN 0-395-68132-4   PA ISBN 0-395-79725-X
        1. Magdalenian culture—France—Juvenile fiction.
[1. Magdalenian culture—France—Fiction.   2. Man,
Prehistoric—Fiction.]   I. Title.
PZ7.C8377Dar   1994
[Fic]—dc20   93-17200
                                                CIP
                                                AC

VB   10   9   8   7   6   5   4   3

My bone-deep gratitude to a small,
lively clan of family and friends
who have given their time, honesty,
and encouragement to *Dar* and me.

Contents

Foreword

Dar and the Spear-Thrower is the story of a boy living fifteen thousand years ago in the region we now call France. The background of the story is based on the archaeological record and current research on this rich period of human prehistory.

Dar and the people of his time are known to us as Cro-Magnons. Although their lives were very different from ours, their brains were as large and complex as our own. With this high intelligence, they produced remarkable cave paintings, sculpture, jewelry, tools, and weapons—such as the spear-thrower.

Although Europe in the Upper Paleolithic period was still in the grip of the Ice Age, there were intervals of milder weather. Dar lived during one of those intervals.

The people in the story inhabited an area called the Massif Central in southeastern France. It is a land filled with steep limestone cliffs, narrow valleys, rivers, and broad expanses of rich grassland that once supported great herds of bison, antelope, reindeer, and horse.

We know from the archaeological record that trade took place among the small bands of Cro-Magnons that lived in the area. Trade items included flint, seashells, mammoth ivory, and ideas. Some things, however, leave no record. *Dar and the Spear-Thrower* is a re-creation of a vanished time in the prehistory of the human race.

1

The Morning Fire

Dar awoke just before dawn. It was cold and dark in the skin tent, and he found it hard to leave the warmth of his fox-fur sleep robe. But he had a job to do.

Dar threw off his robe, picked up the leather pouch that held his precious sunstone, and attached it to his belt. He slipped so quietly out of the family tent that neither his grandmother nor his uncle stirred in their sleep.

Dar hurried to the fire pit in the center of the circle of tents that sheltered the twenty-one members of his clan. Although he was the only person up, Dar did not feel alone. He could hear the hollow hooting of an owl that called out every morning just before daybreak. From one of the tents came the cries of a hungry baby, and from another, loud, insistent snores.

There was another sound, more disturbing. From just outside the camp clearing came the grunts of a scavenging bear. Dar's spear was in his tent, but he was confident he had another way to keep the bear from entering the camp.

Quickly opening his waist pouch, Dar first pulled out a handful of dry moss and put it in the fire pit. Then he took out two small rocks. One was flinty gray. The other rock, the sunstone, was dull yellow and had a deep groove down its center. It was this remarkable stone that made Dar feel secure. Holding the sunstone in his left hand, Dar struck it hard and repeatedly with the flint rock. Sparks flew from the fire rocks, and the air was filled with the familiar acrid smell. Finally, some of the sparks fell on the moss and began to smolder there.

The grunts were louder; the bear was close. Dar couldn't see it in the predawn darkness, but he smelled the animal's pungent odor.

Dar cupped his hands around the moss and blew on it until the glowing tinder burst into flame. Blowing steadily, Dar fed twigs to the fire. When they began to burn, he added dry branches. When the branches flared, lighting up the tents and surrounding trees, Dar caught a glimpse of the bear as it turned and lumbered away from the clearing. Dar smiled with satisfaction. The bear was afraid of his fire.

As Dar was putting the fire rocks back into his waist pouch, the sunstone glowed briefly as it caught the reflection of the flames. Dar gave silent thanks to his dead grandfather for the shiny yellow rock. Many years ago, long before Dar was born, his grandfather had traded two mammoth tusks to a stranger in exchange for the sunstone. Until the time of the trade, the clan had used the friction of wood against wood to start fires. Striking flint against the sunstone had proved to be so much quicker and more reliable that now everyone in the clan had sunstones. It had taken many years to collect them. They were not easy to find.

It was a clan tradition that a boy nearing his manhood was chosen for the task of getting up before the others and starting the morning fire. When Dar was made responsible for this job, his grandmother had given him his grandfather's treasured sunstone.

Until Dar's people awoke and joined him at the fire pit, this dark and quiet time was his own. He always used it in the same way. He picked up a chunky scrap of wood and then looked for a sharp flint chip to use as a carving tool. He found one quickly. The ground around the hearth was littered with flint chips left from the toolmaking that took place around the fire.

What should he carve? Could he capture the look of a red deer with its head held high in panic, perhaps running from a wolf pack? Dar sat by the snapping fire and worked on his carving with such intensity that he almost forgot to breathe. Or to listen.

"Not a bad fire, Dar. This is the one task you've learned well."

Startled by the voice of his uncle, Kenok, Dar let the flint chip fall to the ground and tried to hide the carving behind his back. Kenok loomed above him, and Dar felt small and insignificant next to this tall, black-bearded man.

Kenok was up early for a hunting trip. He carried two flint knives in his belt, and three spears rested on his muscled shoulder. A long time ago, his manmark—five short, parallel lines—had been cut into his upper left arm. Dar looked hard at the mark. He, too, would receive the clan's emblem of manhood at his initiation ceremony.

Kenok held out his hand. "Another carving? Let me see it." Reluctantly, Dar handed over the half-finished piece. Kenok spoke with irritation. "What's the point of doing this?" Dar started to speak, but Kenok cut him off. "We don't need a carver. This clan needs a hunter, a toolmaker, a provider. We can't eat a carving." He thrust the piece back at Dar and spoke in a tight voice. "You and Bowan have lived through thirteen winters, and now your initiation ceremony is coming soon. Bowan seems ready. . . . I'm not sure you are. The shaman said the ceremony will take place in the sacred cave at the next dark of the moon."

Dar tensed. So soon? He tried to speak in a natural tone. "After the ceremony, Uncle, I'll be allowed to hunt with you and the others."

"That's true, you'll join the men," Kenok said. "But you've spent too much time play-hunting with the younger boys and not enough time working with flint. Bowan is your age, but he's a far better toolmaker than you are. Yet you show no interest in learning what I have to teach you. Your fire-making days will soon be over and this job will go to a younger boy. Dar, you have much to learn before your initiation." Kenok picked up his spears. "The other hunters are waiting for me at the river. Think about what I've said. It's time for you to grow up." Kenok turned and strode off.

Dar wasn't eager to think about what his uncle had said. He didn't want to give up making the morning fire or his carving. And he was full of fears about how good a hunter he would be. But after the initiation ceremony, he would be a man among men. To grow up also meant that he would be free from Kenok's power.

2

Spirit Cat

The clanpeople began to straggle out of the five tents that circled the fire pit. They headed toward the morning fire, and their talk and laughter made their breath steam in the cold air. The coming of warmer weather allowed the clan to gather together to eat and make plans for the day. In the colder seasons, each family ate alone inside its own tent.

Mora, Dar's grandmother, was the first to approach the fire pit. Her long white hair fell down her back, and her gray-green eyes were deeply set in her wrinkled face. Mora nodded to her only grandchild. "I don't know if I could make myself get up from my sleep robe without this fire." She noticed Dar's troubled face. "Kenok must have stopped here before going off on his hunt," she said quietly.

Dar gave a short nod and folded his arms. He wasn't ready to talk about his uncle's visit.

Everyone watched as Mora started to prepare the

first meal of the day. Two girls returned from the river with a water-filled skin bag attached to a carrying pole. Mora poured the water into a large wooden pot. From a nearby underground storage pit she took shredded, smoked reindeer meat and a marrow bone and put them into the pot. She added grassy herbs.

With a horn spoon, Mora scooped up some of the red-hot river cobbles that lined the fire pit and dropped them into the water. The clanpeople continued talking as they waited for the soup to cook, heated by the stone pot boilers.

Everyone waited for Mora's reaction as she took the first spoonful. "A little watery, and onions would have helped the flavor, but the storage pit is almost empty. We must go on a gathering walk after the meal," she said.

When Mora spoke, even the hunters paid attention. She was the oldest member of the clan and she knew every fruit, herb, flower, root, and tree. Mora could tell which plants could be eaten safely, which could soften leather or heal wounds, and which river reeds made the best baskets. Mora's experience and memory played a vital role in the well-being of her people.

After the morning meal, the women and children returned to the tents to get their leather carrying bags. The three women with infants got out their back slings and put their babies in them for the walk.

When Dar returned to his family tent, he found Mora with her carrying bag on her shoulder and her digging stick in her hand. "What's the matter, Dar?" she asked. "Don't you want to go with us?"

Dar was not surprised at his grandmother's ability to know his moods; she had cared for him since he was a baby. His father had been killed on a hunt just before Dar was born. His mother had died shortly after Dar's birth.

Dar reached for the carrying bag Mora held out for him. "I like gathering walks. But this may be my last one."

"Yes," Mora said. "You'll soon leave the gathering to the women and children and join the hunters."

"Grandmother, I know the ceremony is coming soon," Dar said. "Uncle told me this morning that it would take place at the next dark of the moon. I want to be a man—but I don't understand how I'll suddenly become one." Dar looked away from Mora. "I don't know if I'm tall enough or strong enough. And Uncle thinks I don't know enough to be a man." Dar faced his grandmother. "He always acts disappointed in me."

"Dar, you and Kenok have problems getting along with each other," Mora said.

"He never smiles at me," Dar said. "Mostly he seems angry. Has he always been like this?"

Mora hesitated before she answered. "No, Kenok changed. He was a lot like you when he was your age. Something happened that changed him."

"Was it the death of my father?" Dar asked.

Mora shook her head. "It wasn't just that your father was killed. It was the strange kind of animal that killed him. Kenok told us a large cat, as big as a lion, jumped on your father and slashed at him with the two long, sharp teeth that hung like daggers from its upper jaw. It happened so fast neither your father nor Kenok could strike back. The cat left as quickly as it had come."

"Uncle won't talk to me about what happened," Dar said.

"No one had ever seen such a cat as Kenok described," Mora said. "He stopped talking about the attack to anyone. That's when he changed. He became serious, almost separate from the rest of us." She shoved her digging stick into her bag. "Just after the attack, Kenok told me he thought the cat was a spirit creature sent to test him as a hunter, as a man."

Dar stared at his grandmother. He began to question her, but Mora held up her hand. "Enough, the others are waiting. We have a long walk ahead of us."

3

The Rocky Ledge

Fourteen women and children were waiting for Mora at the bend of the river, and she led them away from camp along the riverbank. Dar and Bowan, the two oldest boys, acted as guards and carried their spears. The walk was brisk. The younger children scrambled to keep up, but the babies, lulled by the steady rhythm of their mothers' walking, slept in their slings.

Useful plants and animals had been plentiful when the clan first moved into the area. Now, after living there for many seasons, both hunters and gatherers had to travel far from camp to find enough food to sustain the clan.

After a long walk, Mora pointed to a cluster of thin green onions growing near the riverbank. "Look over there," she said. "Tonight's meal will be tasty." The tender shoots were quickly pulled and stored in the bags.

When hunting was poor, squirrels, marmots, and lemmings were welcome additions to the stewpot, and everyone looked for the small animals. The children were responsible for collecting tinder and firewood, both essential for warmth and cooking.

The walk continued until Mora stopped again and prodded the ground with her digging stick. "Tubers underground here. Good for thickening stew, and they can be stored for a long time." Mora worked her stick into the earth searching for the tubers, and the others did the same.

All morning, under Mora's direction, the group searched and collected whatever could be found. The bags filled up with wood, moss, grasses, roots and tubers, reeds, onions, and mushrooms.

A little girl ran up to Mora with a handful of green berries and asked her if they were good to eat.

"They're too hard and sour to eat now," Mora told her. "But the berries will be ripe by summer and then we'll have all we want."

Mora suddenly stopped and pointed to a clump of purple flowers growing high above them on a rocky ledge that jutted out near the top of a cliff. "I haven't seen that plant for three summers. When its flowers and leaves are ground up and mixed with bone marrow, the paste makes a fine medicine to put on wounds. Let's get them all."

Bowan stepped forward. "I'll go up."

"No, Dar will get them," Mora said in a firm voice.

Dar's stomach tightened. *Grandmother knows I'm afraid of heights,* he thought. *Bowan is afraid of nothing, so why doesn't she let him make the climb?* But Dar's silent look of appeal to Mora was met by a blank stare.

Dar handed his spear to Bowan without looking at him. The rugged face of the limestone cliff rose before him. Dar walked to the base and started the climb. It soon became so steep he had to use his hands to cling to the cliff. A rock broke off in his grasp when he approached the halfway point. It clattered down the face of the cliff and crumbled into pieces. Dar looked down and saw the gathering group far below him. They were all looking up at him and seemed as small as deerskin dolls. He felt sick to his stomach.

Dar raised his eyes to the flowering plant still high above him. He ran his tongue over his dry lips and swallowed hard. From above, Dar heard the angry cries of hawks. It was the nesting season. "I'm not here to hurt your chicks," Dar called out to two birds circling overhead.

Dar reached up with his right hand and found another handhold, but he couldn't find a new place to put his left foot. His body trembled. Fear made him unable to move in any direction. Dar clung helplessly to the face of the cliff.

He heard a faint voice from below. "Dar, forget the plants," his grandmother called. "Come down."

Dar was grateful for permission to stop the climb but embarrassed to do so in front of the group. He imagined Bowan's small smile of contempt.

The climb down was more difficult than the trip up. Dar was constantly aware of the ground far beneath him. Pausing to catch his breath, his attention was caught by figures in the distance. Were they humans or animals? Dar shielded his eyes from the sun and saw that it was his uncle's hunting party. The men were walking so slowly they hardly seemed to be moving. One of the hunters was injured; the other two men were having trouble supporting him.

Dar's heart raced as he continued his climb down the cliff. "Something's gone wrong!" he shouted. "A hunter is hurt!"

4

Healing Plants

Dar got down from the cliff and started to run in the direction of the hunting party. He stumbled and fell on the loose rocks that lay near the base of the cliff. He got up and began to run again. By the time he came upon the hunters, he was drenched in sweat and short of breath. Two men struggled to hold up the third man, his uncle.

Dar was startled by Kenok's appearance. Blood covered his torn right shoulder and left thigh, and his right arm hung limply at his side. "What happened, Uncle?" Dar gasped.

Kenok spoke with difficulty. "Bison, a big male . . . I came in close for the spear throw. He charged . . . hooked me with his horns."

Dar could not take his eyes from the bloody wounds. "Will you be all right?" Dar asked in a thin voice. Kenok did not reply. The two other hunters shook their heads in concern.

Dar was relieved to see his grandmother hurrying toward them, followed by the others in the gathering party. Mora's face was creased with worry. She cut off a piece of her tunic and held it tightly against Kenok's bleeding shoulder.

"Grandmother," Dar said, "I'm going back up to get the healing plants!" He started for the cliff at a run before she could speak. "I'll meet you in camp," he shouted.

At the base of the cliff, Dar looked up at the purple flowers high above him. One hawk was perched on the ledge beside them. The other bird soared on its broad wings high above the ledge.

Dar began the climb. He chose his steps and handholds with care. Knowing his fear might over-whelm him again, he tried not to look down. He was soon close to the spot where the rock had given way on his first climb. He slipped his foot into a narrow cleft he hadn't noticed before, but he still needed a good handhold to reach the ledge. He swept his arm overhead and found a protruding rock he hoped would support his weight. It did— he was almost to the ledge. Dar's breath came in painful gulps, but the thought of Kenok's white face and bloody wounds helped keep him going. Dar had never had the opportunity to do anything so important for his uncle—or his clan. It gave him an unfamiliar sense of power.

The hawk on the ledge began to scream. Dar was now close enough to see that the rocky ledge held both the healing plants and a nest with three downy fledglings in it. The second hawk started to drop down from the sky to defend the nest. Dar yelled at the birds, hoping to scare them off.

He pulled himself up to the ledge and looked directly into the furious eyes of a hawk. The screaming, hissing bird came toward him, its wings spread in a fighting stance. When Dar reached for the plants, the hawk slashed him with its talons, piercing the skin on the back of one hand. Dar grabbed the plants near their roots and pulled them free. He shoved them into his shoulder pouch and began his descent. Their young now safe, the hawks fell silent.

On the climb down, Dar was surprised to find he didn't have to think of where to put his hands, his feet, his weight. His body seemed to do the thinking for him.

Dar paused to catch his breath at the base of the cliff, then ran toward camp. "I've got them! I've got the healing plants!" he shouted.

The clanpeople were gathered outside the family tent. Inside, Mora was washing Kenok's wounds. His uncle's eyes were closed and his head lolled to one side.

"Grandmother," Dar said, "where's the marrow?"

Mora pointed toward a shinbone of a deer lying beside her on a flat rock. "We're lucky. This was the last marrow bone in the storage pit."

Mora left Kenok to cut away the meat. Then she brought a heavy rock down on the exposed bone, shattering it to reveal the soft, yellowish, fatty marrow within. Mora spooned the marrow into a small wooden bowl. She took the plants from Dar, discarded the stems, and ground the leaves and flowers together with the rock. She added the plant mix to the marrow in the bowl and worked them into a paste with her fingers.

Mora smeared Kenok's wounds with the salve. "You did a good thing, Dar. Now we can only wait."

As the sky began to darken, Jenu, the shaman, came quietly into the tent and nodded to Mora and Dar. He carried his small sacred drum under his arm. This quiet, withdrawn man lived alone in a small tent set back from the others. Jenu was blind in one eye and had a tremor in his right hand. He could neither hunt nor make tools, but the clan gave the shaman all he needed in gratitude for his spiritual leadership. It was he who knew the sacred songs and stories. And it was he who preserved the ways of the clan in ceremony to guarantee that the natural world remained in balance with the world of spirits.

The shaman sat beside Kenok with his drum between his knees. He looked intently at the injured man for a few moments before he took dark-red ash from his waist pouch and sprinkled it over Kenok's still body. Then Jenu threw back his head and began to chant in a low, pulsating voice. His hands echoed the rhythm of his words on his drum. Dar had heard the shaman chant the legends of his clan many times, but now he found the words impossible to understand. The song seemed to be sung for the world of spirits.

Jenu sat crouched over his drum, playing and chanting until it was dark inside the tent. Then he stopped and seemed to shake himself into wakefulness. He stood up. "Mora, I have delivered the message to the other world." The shaman left as abruptly as he had entered.

Dar lit a fire in the tent's hearth, and he and Mora sat down near Kenok to watch and care for him through the night. When the morning light finally came through the tent skin, they could see that Kenok's bleeding had stopped. Mora smiled at Dar. "You, the healing plants, and the spirits have saved Kenok. Now, get some rest."

Dar shook his head. "I have to build the morning fire first." He got up, reached out to lift the tent flap, and noticed his injured hand. It was now red-streaked where the talons of the hawk had slashed it during his climb. He walked back and rubbed a bit of the salve on his hand. Then he straightened his shoulders and left the tent.

5

Checking Snares

When Dar got to the fire pit, the clanpeople were already there waiting for him. They asked about Kenok and were relieved to hear that his bleeding had stopped. Kenok was the clan's best hunter and his presence would be missed. The four other men always listened closely to his ideas about how to get the meat, skins, and furs necessary to clothe and feed the clan. In the end, after discussion and argument, they usually agreed with Kenok's suggestions.

Dar ate a hurried meal with the others and then returned to his uncle's side. Kenok was awake but his face was tight with pain. Mora was putting the last of the healing salve on his wounds.

Dar nodded to his uncle and put on his shoulder pouch. "I'm going to look for more healing plants today."

Mora gestured her approval. "My mother was told by her grandmother that the medicine works best if it's made from fresh leaves and flowers."

Kenok shook his head. "Dar, you're needed for another job. It would be fine if you found more of the plants, but their work is done. I'm no longer bleeding." Kenok took the bowl of steaming water and deer fat Mora offered him. "I had planned to check and reset my snares in the pine forest today. I want you to do it for me. There are five snares. Head into the forest just beyond the second rapid up the river."

Dar forgot his sleepless night. Kenok had given him an important task to do. "I'll leave right away, Uncle."

"It's a half-day walk to the forest. Be back by sundown," Kenok said. "I don't want you walking alone in the dark."

Mora took the pile of deer meat she had removed from the shinbone the day before and wrapped it in wet leaves. "Take this for your midday meal."

Dar put the meat into his shoulder pouch. He picked up a wooden club and his spear and turned to leave.

Kenok frowned at him. "Is your spearpoint sharp?"

Dar grinned. "Sharp enough for emptying snares and hunting plants." He waved and left the tent before his uncle could reply.

Dar started out along the riverbank and hurried through the familiar territory of his clan. When he reached the first rapid, he saw three suspended basket traps. They were positioned to catch salmon as the fish migrated up the river to spawn. There were salmon in all the baskets. Today, Dar left them to be emptied by the younger children.

The riverbank was wet and slippery from the spray of the rapid and Dar had to slow down. When he reached the second rapid, the sun was almost overhead, but it was shrouded in fog and gave little warmth. He turned and headed for the pine forest. The forest was part of his clan's hunting territory, but he had never been there alone.

It was hard to find the snares in the dim light. Dar was drawn to the first snare by the yelps of a fox that dangled by one leg from a noose attached to a pine sapling. He silenced it with one hard blow of his club. He removed the fox from the noose and admired its pelt.

To reset the snare, Dar pulled the sapling down far enough so the noose could be looped over a bone on the ground. He replaced the heavy rock that held both the noose and the bone in position. When an animal walked into the noose to pull at the bone, the snare would be tripped. The sapling would spring upright and the animal would be caught in the tightening noose.

The next snare was empty, but the third held a half-eaten fox with the noose around its neck.

There were bear tracks on the ground. Dar removed the mangy, worm-infested animal and threw it aside. The sun was now directly overhead, still veiled by fog. He reset the snare and hurried on.

The fourth snare was empty, but Dar heard whining from the fifth trap up ahead. When he got there, walking more slowly with the fox draped over his shoulder, he found the snare had trapped a fox cub.

Dar put down his burdens. "You're too little to be off by yourself," he said to the struggling fox. "Calling for your mother won't help you now." Dar picked up the cub by the scruff of its neck and looked into the eyes of the terrified animal. He loosened the noose around its leg. "All right, go." The little fox dropped to the ground and ran off into the underbrush. *Uncle would not have released the cub,* Dar thought, *but I'm glad I did.*

As Dar bent to gather up his gear he heard a sudden crackling of leaves behind him. He jumped. He picked up his spear and ducked behind a tree trunk. After waiting a moment, he carefully peered from behind the tree. A heavily bearded stranger was walking rapidly toward him.

6

The Stranger

◁

The man was about the same age as Kenok, but not nearly as tall or muscular. The stranger had a manmark of two crossed short lines on his cheek. He carried his spear at his side, its spearpoint made of antler instead of flint. Unlike Dar's people, who wore smooth skins during the warmer seasons, the man was dressed in a fur tunic. The fur was reddish brown, the same color as the stranger's hair and beard. It gave him the look of a shaggy animal.

Dar's legs felt weak. What was this man doing here? Was he alone? Dar tightened his grip on his spear, but wished he had sharpened his spearpoint before leaving home.

Noticing Dar's shoulder pouch, the man stopped. He picked up the bag, quickly dropped it, then lifted his spear above his shoulder. His nostrils flared and his eyes scanned the area.

Dar drew back behind the tree, but as he did so his spear made a small scraping sound against the bark. The stranger must have heard it. Dar's mouth was so dry he couldn't swallow. This man was fit, alert, and well armed. It would be reckless to challenge him.

Dar stepped from behind the tree, his spear with its point downward in his left hand. The crouching stranger faced him with his spear poised, ready to throw. The man glared at him and spoke in a harsh-sounding language that Dar didn't understand.

Shaking, Dar took one step forward and raised his empty right hand to show the man he meant him no harm. The stranger stood up from his crouch but kept his spear raised. Again, the strange words. Dar shook his head and shrugged to let the stranger know he did not speak his language.

Dar felt he had to make a friendly gesture. He pointed to his pack and slowly walked to it. Removing the deer meat, he held it out toward the furry stranger. The man's eyes narrowed with suspicion as he unwrapped the fresh meat and smelled it. He nodded curtly and returned the meat to Dar.

The stranger put his spear down by his side and opened his own shoulder pouch. He took out a hand-size piece of wood with a groove down its center, and a small, sharp wooden stick. He knelt down and placed a piece of dried fungus from his pouch on the grooved wood. Then he took the pointed stick, pressed it into the groove of the wooden piece on the ground, and twirled it rapidly between the palms of his hands.

Dar had never seen fire sticks being used before, although he knew that long ago his people had started their fires with them. He watched the man struggle to start his fire. The fungus would not smoke, and the stranger muttered in irritation. *It must be the mist in the forest,* Dar thought. The friction between the fire sticks would not produce enough heat to start a fire.

Dar took out his fire rocks. The sunstone caught a dim ray of sunlight, and the stranger stiffened and stared at the flashing rock. Dar replaced the man's fungus on the ground. The stranger watched Dar's every move. Dar struck the fire rocks together over the fungus. When sparks fell on the tinder and ignited it, the man's head snapped back and he snorted in astonishment.

Dar fed the little flame with pine needles and then small, dry branches. He started to put his fire rocks away, but the man held out his hand. Dar hesitated, then let the stranger examine the rocks. The man was only interested in the sunstone. He sniffed it and wrinkled his nose over its acrid smell.

Dar took back the fire rocks and returned them to his pouch. He skewered the meat on two green branches and handed one to the stranger. They roasted the meat over the fire and ate their meal in silence.

When they finished, the man licked his fingers clean and then pointed to Dar's waist pouch. Dar regretted showing the stranger his precious sunstone and shook his head.

The man reached into his own pouch and brought out a slim rod of reindeer antler. It was as long as Dar's forearm, with a handle carved on one end and a pointed hook on the other. Dar had never seen anything like it. The stranger thrust it into Dar's hands, and Dar saw that a leaping horse had been carved on one end of the rod. The horse's front legs were folded against its chest and its back legs were straight.

Dar had never imagined that a carving could be so beautiful. He thought of his own work and realized how crude it was. What was this rod? Was it a sacred object worshiped by the stranger's clan? Or had it been carved, like his own efforts, to capture a moment in the life of an animal, and nothing more?

The man took back the rod. He picked up his spear and pointed to a fallen tree many strides away. Could he hurl it so far? Even Kenok, the strongest man in Dar's clan, could throw a spear only half the distance. And the stranger was a head shorter than Kenok.

The man pointed to the tree again. Then he held his rod of antler over and behind his shoulder, hook end up, and laid his spear along the rod so the spear pointed forward and the hook caught the butt end of the spear. The stranger glanced at Dar, smiled for the first time, and leaned far back for the throw. He brought his body and arm rapidly forward, snapping his wrist and launching the spear with tremendous force and speed.

Dar, open-mouthed, watched the hurtling arc of the spear and saw it plunge into the target tree. The whole process had happened so fast and so smoothly it took Dar a moment to realize that the antler rod remained in the stranger's hand.

The man retrieved his spear and came back to where Dar stood. Again he pointed to Dar's waist pouch. With his other hand he held out the throwing rod. Dar's body was tense with indecision. His grandfather's sunstone was his most valued possession; he could not trade it away. Dar shook his head in refusal.

The stranger frowned, then tucked the rod into his belt. He tapped his chest. "Toreg," he said several times and pointed to two tall mountains behind the pine forest. Then he drew the twin peaks in the dirt with his finger and pointed to the valley between them. He added a rough circle near the mountains and spoke a word that sounded to Dar like his own clan's word for lake.

Dar studied the mountains before him and Toreg's drawing on the ground. He touched his own chest and said, "Dar." Toreg pointed again to his antler rod and to Dar's waist pouch. Then he gave Dar a short, raised-hand salute, and walked away toward the mountains.

Dar followed the stranger with his eyes until he disappeared. He would have to run most of the way home to be back in camp by sundown. He put the fox back over his shoulder and secured its legs together in front by a leather thong. He picked up his gear and started for home.

Had he made a mistake in refusing the trade, Dar asked himself. Perhaps he had. He prized his grandfather's sunstone, but after many years of searching, his clan knew where to look for the shiny yellow rocks. If he owned the magical rod with the carved horse on it, it wouldn't matter anymore that he was short. With the rod, he would be the equal of any hunter in his clan.

Dar thought of nothing but Toreg and the spear-thrower all the way home.

7

Beginnings

Dar returned to camp just after the day turned dark. He was greeted by the welcome smell of roasting meat. The hunters must have had a successful day even without his uncle. Dar hurried to his tent and found Kenok sitting up on his sleep robe. Mora sat beside him.

"I'm glad you're back, Dar," she said.

Kenok gave Dar a hard look from under his heavy brow ridges. "I told you to be here before dark."

Dar removed the fox from his shoulder and handed it to Mora. "I know. I have something to tell you both."

Kenok ignored what Dar had said. "Only one? I'm surprised."

"Two snares were empty," Dar said. "And one held a half-eaten, mangy fox I had to throw away."

"So, where's the fifth catch?" Kenok asked.

Dar did not return Kenok's gaze. "I let a fox cub go."

"What a wasteful thing to do," Kenok said. "That fur is soft. . . . Good for a hat, children's boots, lots of things."

"Uncle, the fox was just a baby," Dar said. "It deserved a chance to grow up."

His grandmother looked sharply at his uncle.

Kenok spoke to Dar but stared at Mora while he talked. "I think you acted foolishly, like a woman." Mora and Kenok glared at each other in a way that Dar had never seen. Kenok pulled himself away with effort and turned to Dar. "Did you reset the traps at least?"

Dar spoke quickly to try to break the tension he didn't understand. "Yes, well, all but the last trap. I was about to reset it when something happened."

"What happened?" Kenok demanded.

Dar took a deep breath. "I met a stranger just after I released the cub. He was a man of your age, Uncle."

Kenok jerked his head up. "What was he doing in our territory?"

"I don't know," Dar said. "We couldn't understand each other. He was dressed in fur and his spearpoint was made of antler."

"Dressed in fur?" Mora asked in alarm. "Did he seem dangerous? Were you frightened of him?"

"At first. And he was frightened of me. I startled him," Dar said. "He had his spear ready to throw.

I offered him some of my deer meat to show I meant him no harm. He tried to start a fire with his fire sticks, but it was so misty in the forest, they wouldn't work. So I used my fire rocks and got a fire going."

Kenok nodded impatiently. "Then what happened?"

"He had never seen a sunstone before, and he wanted it." Kenok's face tightened, but Dar continued, his voice filling with enthusiasm. "Then he showed me something I've never seen. It's a rod made of antler with a beautiful horse carved on it. I call it a spear-thrower because when a spear is attached to the hooked end of the rod, it makes the throw longer and faster than a spear thrown without it."

Kenok spoke in a sneering tone. "And how do you know what this spear-thrower can do?"

Dar leaned forward. "He showed me how it works! With the spear-thrower, his spear went twice as far as any I've ever seen. And he's a short man, Uncle, and not as strong as you."

Kenok said nothing for a long time. Then he shook his head. "It's not our way."

Dar looked at his uncle's scowling face and had trouble forcing out the words. "It's a better way."

Kenok's eyes darkened. "You didn't trade your grandfather's sunstone for it, did you?"

"No, Uncle, I didn't," Dar said. "But maybe I should have."

"I can't believe you even considered doing such a thing," Kenok said angrily.

"The sunstone is mine to trade," Dar said. "Grandmother gave it to me."

"You don't deserve to have it," Kenok said, his voice rising. "It was my father's. If she'd given it to me, I would never let it go!" Kenok's eyes closed briefly. "Leave me. I don't want to listen to your childish talk."

Without a word, Dar left the tent. He paused outside and heard his grandmother and uncle talking in low, angry voices. Dar walked to his favorite boulder and sat on its smooth face. In the cold night, it still held the warmth of the sun. Dar sat hugging his legs, his chin resting on his knees.

After a while, Mora came out of the tent holding a beaver-fur cape around her shoulders with one hand and an animal-fat lamp with the other. "Come back and sleep, Grandson. You've had a long day."

Dar made no move to leave the rock. He looked at Mora and saw for the first time how bent her back was and how gnarled and misshapen her fingers were. Dar had always thought of his grandmother as strong and vital. He had refused to see that she was aging.

"Why did you and Uncle get so angry at each

other?" Dar asked. "It seemed to start when I told him about the fox cub."

Mora put her lamp on the boulder and sat next to Dar. "It goes far back, just before you were born. Your father had just been killed. Your mother was sorrowing and weak, not eating enough. It was a difficult time for the clan. Hunting was poor. We were going to move camp as soon as you were born. Your birthing was hard. The clan waited for your mother to recover, but she never got back her strength, never got up from her sleep robe."

Dar shivered in the cold night. "And then she died?"

"Yes, and your uncle was sure you couldn't live without her milk," Mora said. "He didn't want a sickly newborn, without father or mother, to be a part of the move to a new camp."

Dar had never heard this part of his story. "What happened?"

"I argued with him," Mora said. "I told him we should break camp at once, and that I would be responsible for you as well as for doing my share of the work. I prepared a special gruel of ground roots, eggs, and honey and fed it to you whenever you cried. It was a long and difficult walk. No one thought you would live through it. But you did."

Dar was silent for a long time. Finally he said, "So he was angry at me for being a crying, demanding baby, interfering with the plans of the clan."

Mora turned her head away. "Kenok never said that."

Dar thought of something for the first time. "Why did you give the sunstone to me instead of Uncle?"

"You had lost so much," Mora said. "Both mother and father. I wanted to give you something from your past. When you were put in charge of the morning fire, it seemed the right time to do it."

"Grandmother, you've been telling me things I've never heard before," Dar said. "Why?"

"You're about to become a man, Dar. It's time you learned about your beginnings." Mora got down from the boulder and picked up her lamp. "I'm going to sleep. Are you coming?"

"Soon," Dar answered. He had a lot to think about and wanted to return to the tent after both his uncle and grandmother were asleep.

8

Intruder

◁

D ar sat alone beside his fire in the cold dawn. He hugged his knees and thought about the sliver of moon that had hung in the sky last night. The coming initiation ceremony made him aware of the passage of time in a new and troubling way. Soon the moon would disappear from view and the dark of the moon would be here. And with it would come the ceremony.

Dar thought about the ritual that would somehow change him into a man—and shivered. For warmth and comfort, he made a hot broth of water and some dried mushrooms he found in the storage pit. Near the pit he noticed a stretched deerskin secured to the ground by sharp wooden pegs. He returned to his worries by the fire.

When a tent flap opened, Dar looked up and watched his grandmother walk to the fire. It was rare to have anyone join him this early, and she had never done it before.

"It's cold, Grandmother," Dar said, and handed Mora his drink to share. "Why are you up so early?"

Mora knelt down by the stretched deerskin. "You and Kenok both need new tunics, and it takes me longer than ever to get the skins ready for sewing. Bending over is hard on my back, so I thought I'd start early and work for shorter periods of time." Using a flat flint tool, Mora began to scrape the blood, fat, and scraps of muscle from the exposed underside of the deerskin.

Dar watched her sure strokes. "Grandmother, the ceremony is almost here. If I tell you something, will you promise not to tease me?" Her kind face made him continue. "I'm frightened. What if I fail at something during the ceremony and they don't think I deserve to be a man?"

"Every boy is frightened before his initiation ceremony," Mora said.

Dar looked into the fire. "I don't think Bowan is."

Mora shook her head. "*Every* boy is frightened," she repeated.

"Was my father afraid?" Dar asked.

"Of course," Mora said. "And so was your uncle." *Kenok frightened!* Dar felt better.

"Dar, the real test is whether you can do what is expected of you even if you have fears and doubts about yourself," Mora said.

Dar thought of the rocky ledge. "Was that why you sent me, instead of Bowan, to get the healing plants?"

Mora looked up and nodded, then suddenly shouted, "Behind you—bear!"

Dar spun around to see a large brown bear standing on its hind legs with its snout lifted to catch the scent of Mora's deerskin. Dar, as usual, had left his spear in the tent, too confident of animals' inborn fear of fire. The smell of fresh blood and fat had overcome the bear's fear.

The bear dropped to the ground and started toward the deerskin in a slow, stiff-legged walk, its head swaying from side to side. Dar had never been this close to a large and hungry bear. He grabbed the unlit end of a flaming piece of firewood and put himself between the intruder and his grandmother. The bear rose again on its hind legs, and Dar saw clearly the long, curved claws that he must avoid.

Dar walked toward the bear, shouting and waving the torch in front of its face. The bear ignored the torch and moved closer to the deerskin. Then Dar came in close and pushed the torch directly into its snout. The bear let out a roar, dropped down, and whirled around on its back legs. It lunged off into the trees beyond the camp clearing, leaving the smell of singed flesh and fur in the cold air.

Hearing the commotion, the clanpeople spilled out of their tents, the men with weapons in their hands, the women clutching their children. Dar looked at the startled faces around him and waited for his grandmother to say something, but she nodded to him. Dar spoke. "A large bear with a burned nose, but he's gone."

Mora whispered to Dar, "You see, you acted even though you were frightened." In a louder voice she said, "I'm going to prepare the morning meal. Dar will have a large portion."

9

Dark of the Moon

◁—————————————————————————

While Dar waited for the initiation ceremony, he never stopped thinking about the stranger and his spear-thrower. He wanted the magical antler rod more with each passing day. *The ceremony will make me a man,* Dar thought. *The spear-thrower will make me a magnificent hunter.* After the ceremony, he would be able to do what he wanted without his uncle's permission. He would go to the stranger's camp to make the trade he had refused in the pine forest.

After the morning meal, Dar and Bowan were sent to a lookout post high above the valley floor to watch for reindeer herds that would soon enter the valley in search of spring grasses. They could see no clouds of dust in the distance, and returned to camp. In the afternoon, all the boys went spear fishing in the river. The fish were wily, and Bowan speared the only salmon caught.

That night, Dar could find no moon when he searched the sky. He felt the hair on the back of his neck rise. The ceremony was upon him. Later, in the tent, anxious in his sleep robe, Dar got up and went outside to look again. It was the dark of the moon.

When Dar returned to the tent, he could tell by his uncle's breathing that he was awake. Dar went over to Kenok to tell him the moon had disappeared. Before Dar could speak, Kenok said, "I know. Are you ready, Dar?"

"I think so, Uncle," Dar said in a low voice, and returned to his bedding.

Dar spent a fitful night twisting and turning. In a dream he saw himself as a younger boy watching a strange animal by moonlight. It had the belly of a pregnant mare, the legs of a lion, and two straight, long horns that jutted forward from its forehead. The creature bit off and swallowed a sliver of the moon, then turned to Dar with its mouth open. Dar awoke, covered with sweat.

He could tell by the pale color of the tent skin that it was close to sunrise. Dar got up and went to the fire pit. He made his last morning fire slowly and with great care. As the flames leaped up, the shaman came to the fire pit, followed by Bowan.

"You two are to eat nothing until the new moon returns to the sky and you are reborn as men," Jenu said. He pointed to an oak tree. "When the sun hits the top of that tree, your walk to the sacred cave must begin. When you reach the cave, enter it and move toward the light at its heart." Dar had never heard Jenu speak so sternly. "Now, go to the river and immerse yourselves. The water will cleanse you of your childhood." The shaman turned and left them.

Bowan led the way to the river at a fast pace. Over his shoulder, he called out to Dar, "Hurry up! This is the first step of our initiation ceremony!"

Dar walked faster, but stopped when he saw small ice chunks floating in the river. "Bowan, we're going to freeze in this water!"

"Come on, Dar," Bowan said, already taking off his tunic and boots. "It's what we have to do."

Dar reluctantly took off his clothes and followed Bowan into the frigid water. He ducked under the surface in order to prevent himself from crying out with the shock of the cold on his body.

After a moment, Dar and Bowan scrambled out of the river, picked up their clothing, and ran naked back to camp. When they reached the hearth, the fire was almost out. They quickly built it up again, dressed, and moved close to the flames to warm themselves.

They waited for the clanpeople to join them, but it slowly became apparent that there were no men in camp. Mora and the other women were silent as they prepared the morning meal for themselves and the children; he and Bowan would receive no food. Dar's grandmother would not even look at him as she went about her work. This was a day for the men of the clan.

A few of the children started a game of play-hunt around the hearth after they'd eaten, pretending to stalk a woolly rhinoceros. Dar longed to be a part of the game, but he did as Bowan was doing and sat close to the fire, silently staring into the flames.

Bowan finally looked up at the oak tree on the hill. Its crown was struck with sunlight. "It's time!" he said.

Dar envied Bowan's confident tone. Leaving behind the women and children, they started the walk to the sacred cave.

10

The Sacred Cave

All the clanpeople knew the location of the sacred cave, but this was the first time Dar and
Bowan had been summoned there. Even as a young
boy Dar had lowered his voice when he passed its
dark entrance. He knew important ceremonies
were held inside, but no adult had ever told the
children the secrets of the cave.

Bowan took the lead on the narrow trail leading
to the cave and walked with a springy step. "It's
about to happen, Dar! Soon we'll be men." Dar did
not reply.

The sun was overhead by the time they reached
the cave. Bowan stopped in front of its dark entrance and then stood very still, his high spirits suddenly gone.

"Go inside, Bowan," Dar said. "What are you
waiting for?"

Bowan seemed rooted to the ground. "You go
first," he said in a small voice.

Seeing his strained face, Dar pressed Bowan's

shoulder with his hand, then walked past him and ducked into the low cave entrance. Bowan followed close behind.

They were plunged into another world. The narrow entry was cold and clammy. Faint traces of smoke hung in the stale air. The shaman had told them to move toward the light, but there was no light. Dar stretched out his arms to touch the jagged walls, but he could only feel a wall on his left. A stone clattered into the empty darkness on his right. Dar's body was cold as he walked forward in the darkness. The cavern echoed their heavy breathing.

Dar moved slowly to avoid stumbling on the loose gravel on the path. His head struck a rock jutting out from the wall. "Drop down," he whispered to Bowan. They wriggled on their bellies until the overhang was behind them.

A faint glow appeared ahead. Now Dar could see the dangerous drop on the right of the path. As they made their way forward, the glow became brighter. Dar heard the thumping of his heart; surely, Bowan could hear it, too. The beats became louder, faster. *Not heartbeats, drumbeats!* Dar quickened his steps to match the tempo of the drum. Turning a corner, he stopped so suddenly that Bowan bumped into him. They were at the entrance of a large chamber lit by shimmering torchlight. They had found the light at the heart of the cave.

Slowly, Dar took in the spectacle before him. A towering figure of a man stood on a stone platform in the center of the chamber. His white fox-fur cape fell below his knees. Bison horns seemed to grow from his leather head covering. A lion's tooth hung from his gleaming necklace of iridescent seashells. It took Dar a moment to realize this was Jenu who stood before him, transformed and majestic.

The five adult men of Dar's clan were in the chamber. Behind the shaman stood Kenok, holding a spear for support. The pain of his injury still showed in his face. He was dressed in his finest fawnskin tunic and new beaver leggings. Attached to Kenok's belt was a green stone dagger Dar had never seen before.

The shaman jabbed a forefinger at Dar and Bowan. "Come forward!" he said.

In the folds of Jenu's cape Dar saw a splendid flint knife. It was as long as his forearm and thinner than his little finger. The knife was so elegant and fragile, Dar knew it had been made for ceremonial use; a blow would have shattered it.

With a hand wrapped in protective leather, Jenu raised the great knife high above his head. At once, the torchbearers raised their torches on outstretched arms. The upper walls and ceiling of the chamber were bathed in light. Dar sucked in his breath.

Animals leaped across the walls and ceilings of the chamber. Huge wild bulls, outlined in black, lunged forward with energy and power. Galloping black and red horses in furry winter pelts moved in the opposite direction. Antlered deer ran with their heads held high.

Then Dar saw the creature of his dream, the animal with two long, straight horns, the legs of a lion, and the belly of a pregnant mare. In his nightmare, this same creature had come toward him open-mouthed. Was he still dreaming?

Dar stared at the vibrant animals around him. The guardian spirits must have put them there. Or had they been painted to represent the world of animal spirits? Dar stopped questioning, stopped thinking. He was only aware that in the flickering torchlight, the mysterious animals actually seemed to move.

The low, hollow notes of a bone flute began to play. They sounded like the hooting of an owl. The shaman's deep voice joined the flute. From somewhere in the chamber, drumbeats drove the rhythm of his chant:

> *When I speak, the spirits listen,*
> *Give abundance, guard our people.*

When I speak, all creatures listen,
Great bear dances, bison gather.
When I speak, the seasons listen,
White snow melts, red berries ripen.
When I speak, the clan must listen,
Live in balance, all is balance.

Abruptly, the song ended. The flute and drum fell silent. Jenu held his knife out in front of him and spoke. "We are here to determine if these two boys are ready to leave their childhood and become men. They must prove their bravery in front of all the men of this clan. If they show fear or pain, manhood will be denied them."

The shaman pointed to Dar. Hardly breathing, Dar made himself step forward. Jenu bent down and grasped Dar's arm. Dar stared straight ahead. With the knife the shaman cut five short lines, one above the other, into Dar's upper left arm. Blood spilled from the five cuts and they merged into one pain. Then Jenu took white ash from his waist pouch and rubbed it into the manmark. The pain increased. Dar neither flinched nor cried out. The shaman looked into Dar's face, then nodded in approval. Dar felt his chest expand.

The shaman called Bowan to the platform. As Bowan felt the knife his eyes filled with tears. Dar gave him a silent sign of encouragement. The tears did not fall. When it was over, Jenu nodded again and Bowan's shoulders sagged with relief, then straightened. Bowan made a small movement of his head to thank Dar for his support.

The shaman made a quick and unexpected motion and cut a small gash in the palm of his own hand. He flexed his fingers until blood collected in his palm. Then he bent down and mingled his own blood with the blood that flowed from the new manmarks. Now Jenu raised his great knife again and spoke directly to Dar and Bowan:

> *Through me, your blood is merged*
> *With the guardian spirits.*
> *Now you carry within you*
> *All that is sacred to us.*
> *You will come into your manhood*
> *To serve the clan and not yourselves.*
> *When the moon is reborn*
> *From the black womb of the sky,*
> *You two will be reborn as men*
> *And welcomed into this clan.*

The drum began to beat again in a driving rhythm, and now the song of the flute soared above the drums. The shaman began to turn in a tight circle on the stone platform, moving to the powerful drumbeats with the pounding of his feet. Suddenly, Jenu spread his arms wide, and the white fur cape lifted around him like wings. "Dance!" he commanded.

Dar and Bowan began to dance in a circle around the stone platform in the middle of the great painted chamber, their arms streaked with the blood of the clan.

11

Preparations

T wo nights after the ceremony, the moon was still absent from the night sky. Dar was between worlds. His childhood was over. The making of the morning fire was no longer his job; a younger boy had taken his place. But Dar could not participate as an adult in the life of his clan until the dark of the moon had passed.

The shaman had forbidden all food during this waiting period. Dar had never been without food for so long, and there was a dull ache in his stomach. His manmark was painful, but when he was alone, he looked at the mark and admired the slightly raised stripe design. By the summer, the mark would whiten and stand out against his brown arm.

On the third night, Dar saw a thin crescent moon in the sky. The wait was over. The moon had been reborn, and now his new life as an adult could begin.

Dar ate the evening meal in famished gulps.

While the clanpeople were still gathered around the fire listening to the shaman tell a favorite legend, Dar returned to his tent. He built a small fire in the hearth and took down the reed basket that held his few possessions. The new fur boots his grandmother had made for him would be useful on his journey to the stranger's camp. Dar looked closely at three flint spearpoints he had made under Kenok's impatient instruction. They were thick and clumsy; he knew he must do better. He looked again at two of his carvings he had thought were good enough to keep. Compared to the horse on Toreg's spear-thrower, his animals were stiff and lifeless. He threw them in the fire, but could not look as they burned. At the bottom of the basket, he found his father's bone bracelet. He pushed it up to his upper arm, but his muscles were not developed enough to hold it. The bracelet slipped down his arm and fell off.

Mora entered the tent as Dar was transferring the spearpoints and new boots into his shoulder pouch. His first impulse was to hide the pouch from her, but he resisted.

"What are you doing, Dar?" Mora asked.

Dar touched his manmark. "I no longer need Uncle's permission to go, so I'm leaving tomorrow before sunrise to find the stranger's camp." He tried to sound confident. "I'm going to trade my sun-stone for the stranger's spear-thrower."

Mora studied his face; hers was full of worry. "How far is this stranger's camp?"

"I'm not sure," Dar said. "He drew a map in the dirt for me. It might take ten days to get there. I think the camp is in a valley between two mountains with a large lake nearby."

Mora frowned when he mentioned the lake. "How do you know you can trust this man or his people?" she asked, not waiting for an answer. "Many years ago, when my brother was a young man, hunting was poor. He decided to go scouting for a new campsite with good game nearby. I heard my father warn him about a fierce clan that lived near a lake. They looked like animals, and didn't even live in tents." Mora had tears in her voice. "My brother left . . . and never returned. You could be going to the same clan that killed my brother."

Dar stood up—and noticed for the first time that he was the same height as his grandmother. "You don't know he was killed by another clan or even if he was going in the same direction as the clan your father warned him about."

"You may be right," Mora said, "but I fear for you—and for myself. I do not want another loss."

"I can take care of myself," Dar said and returned to his packing. "Don't tell Uncle about my plan, don't tell anyone."

Mora shook her head with irritation. "Kenok will suspect I know where you've gone." She waited for a response, but Dar was silent. "I'll leave food for your journey by your sleep robe." Mora turned quickly to leave the tent, but not before Dar saw that her eyes were filled with tears.

Dar was suddenly overcome with exhaustion and lay down on his bedding. Because he would leave his clan tomorrow, Dar was conscious of the warmth of his heavy robes and the comfort of the snug tent. He breathed in a mixture of smoke, fur, and human smells he would miss. The last thing Dar heard before he fell asleep was the lulling sound of singing coming from the fire pit.

12

The Journey Begins

Dar awoke as usual just before sunrise. He got up quietly and attached his knife and waist pouch to his belt. He was surprised to find his grandmother's deerskin backpack beside his sleep robe. He lifted it to his shoulders and picked up his own shoulder pouch and spear. Dar could tell Mora was only pretending to sleep. He leaned down and whispered, "Thank you, Grandmother." He left the tent without waking his uncle.

At the fire pit, a younger boy was making the morning fire. Dar stopped; perhaps his help was needed. When the boy waved him on, Dar felt a pang of disappointment. He also felt adrift from his secure world. The one he was about to enter was full of worry. How much did he really know about living on his own and keeping himself safe, warm, and fed? He left the camp full of self-doubts.

Dar walked to the river and then retraced his steps to the pine forest. The day was cold and he walked at a rapid pace to build up his body heat.

When Dar reached the place where he had met the stranger, he shrugged off his shoulder pouch and Mora's backpack. Inside the pack he found dried salmon, smoked deer jerky, and freshly washed roots. Mora had also packed her own beaver cape. Dar buried his face in its soft fur. It held his grandmother's scent and made him feel less alone.

Dar sat on a sunlit rock and ate some jerky. Then he searched until he found the exact spot where the stranger had pointed to his camp and drawn a map in the dirt. Dar studied the mountains in front of him, picked up his gear, and started walking in the direction of the twin peaks. He knew they were not as close as they appeared to be.

For the first few days and nights, Dar was overwhelmed with loneliness. He missed the morning reunion of his people around the fire, play-hunting with the other children, listening to stories around the hearth at night. Dar was used to the rhythms of his people, and he had never been so aware of himself as a person apart from his clan.

It became steadily colder as he walked toward the mountains. Dar kept track of the days by cutting notches on a stick. On the third day, he looked into the pack and knew he was eating Mora's food too quickly. He must save some for emergencies and begin to forage for himself.

Late afternoon, on the fourth day of his journey, Dar speared an unwary young deer. He took off a hind leg, skinned it, and roasted it over a fire. No meal had ever tasted better.

While he gnawed at the bone, Dar looked at the body of the deer—and regretted his kill. What could he do with it? The smell of fresh meat would attract wolf, bear, hyena, and lion to his campsite. He couldn't take the time to strip and smoke the deer to make jerky. Dar cooked the remaining three legs to eat in the days ahead, then gathered up his belongings. He reluctantly left the deer's carcass behind and walked away in the dusk to make another campsite.

That night, Dar's sleep was disturbed by the growls of predators fighting over the abandoned deer. From now on, he must rely on small game that could be eaten in a day—or go without meat.

When the weather was good, Dar slept on the ground and woke himself several times during the night to feed the fire; he didn't want hungry or curious animals to visit him while he slept. One rainy, windy night, when building a fire was impossible, Dar climbed a tree and slept in a fork of two branches. He awakened in the cold morning cramped but safe.

On the evening of the eighth day, Dar was striking his fire rocks together to start his evening fire.

He stopped in mid-stroke. After the trade, he would have no way of starting a fire on his trip home. Dar sat very still. Why hadn't he thought his trip through? He could probably get another piece of flint, but a sunstone was difficult to find.

All of Dar's doubts returned. For the first time, he admitted to himself he wasn't sure he could find Toreg's camp. And if he found it, how would he be treated by the stranger and his clan? The story of his great-uncle's disappearance frightened him. Dar considered going home. But he wanted the spear-thrower. With it, he would become a successful hunter, perhaps as good as his uncle. Perhaps better. He must continue his journey.

13

Bone Lake

There were ten notches on Dar's calendar stick when he climbed up a small hill to get a better view of the area. He saw before him a strange sight. Was this the lake Toreg had drawn in the dirt? It didn't move like water. Its dull luster and color reminded him of his father's bone bracelet. He would call it Bone Lake.

Dar came down from the hill and headed toward the shoreline. He touched the surface of the lake with his spear and found that it was frozen solid. In the winter and early spring, the river near his camp carried chunks of ice, but he had never seen anything like this large, motionless body of water.

The two mountain peaks loomed just behind the lake. Dar knew his uncle would tell him to walk around the lake, but why waste the time if he could walk across?

He stepped onto the ice and started off, but he had not anticipated the cold winds that blew over its surface. Dar walked back to shore, exchanged his skin boots for his new fur ones, and put on his grandmother's cape. When he started off again, he walked as quickly as he could to prevent the ice from sticking to the soles of his boots.

Dar was saving time with this shortcut, but when he was nearly halfway across the lake, the ice creaked and shifted beneath his feet. Dar dropped to his hands and knees. The sound continued. He saw cracks in the ice, like streaks of lightning, moving away from him. Abruptly, the thin ice broke through and Dar plunged into the freezing water.

The water closed over his head and soon he felt the icy cold in his very bones. Desperately, Dar began to look for the hole he had fallen through. The breath was being pushed out of his lungs and he felt his energy leaving him. *He could not panic.* He began to move his legs in slow circles to stop himself from sinking.

Dar's lungs ached with the need to breathe. Should he try to get rid of his backpack and shoulder pouch? Why didn't he feel their weight? Dar suddenly understood his good luck: trapped air in the bags was helping to keep him buoyant.

Dar couldn't find the hole he had dropped through. He considered head-butting the ice above him to make another one, but decided against this. He didn't know how thick the ice was and he was afraid of cracking his skull.

Then he felt the shaft of his spear in his numbed hand. He used it to probe above him, looking for a spot of light in the icy black ceiling. Just when Dar thought his lungs would burst, his spear shot through the hole in the ice. He stuck his head through it and greedily gulped in the air.

Dar pushed his waterlogged bags up onto the ice and positioned his spear across the hole. Using the spear to support his weight, Dar lifted and wriggled himself out of the water and onto the frozen surface of the lake. He crawled on his hands and knees across the ice toward the far shore, pushing his gear ahead of him. His whole body was numb. *The pain will come later,* he thought.

Once on shore, Dar lay on the ground hugging himself and shivering in the disappearing sunlight. His breathing was fast and painful and tore at his throat. Dar knew the wind was his enemy. He got up slowly and walked away from the lake, dragging his possessions behind him.

He searched for a boulder large enough still to hold the heat of the sun. He knew he would share it with small animals that would also find its warmth comforting during the night. When he found a boulder, he spread his gear on top of it to dry.

Dar's hands shook badly and were turning white, but he collected dry reeds to serve as tinder for a fire. Out of the worst of the wind, Dar struck the sunstone with the flint. Sparks fell and the reeds smoldered and then caught fire. He added wood and held his hands so close to the fire he almost burned them. Dar huddled near the crackling warmth and once again thanked his grandfather for the sunstone—and wondered if his own trade would prove to be as wise.

After a time, he made a windbreak of dead branches, then gathered together a pile of dry leaves next to the boulder. He lay down on them and covered himself with more leaves. His body slowly warmed, and with the warmth came pain, particularly in his hands, knees, and feet. But Dar was grateful to have survived. He slept, rousing himself only to refuel the fire. Tonight, the fire would keep him not only safe, but alive.

14

▷

Arrival

◁

The next morning, Dar woke up cold and aching. He looked about for signs of large animals and was relieved to find none. He put on his stiff but dry leather tunic and leggings. The fur boots and cape were still wet with lake water, so he attached them to his backpack to dry in the sun.

The twin peaks were directly ahead of him, and he was anxious to reach the stranger's camp before dark. Dar walked until early afternoon, eating some watery jerky he was happy to find at the bottom of his pack.

He stopped at a stand of oak trees and saw two crossed lines that had been carved into a tree trunk, the same mark that Toreg had on his cheek. He had found the way! But now he was a trespasser in the territory of the stranger's clan.

Dar followed a well-traveled path that led out of the stand of oak trees and into a narrow valley. A meandering river flowed through it, and jagged mountains rose up from the valley floor at a sharp angle. Two of the limestone cliffs were taller than the others. These were the twin peaks Toreg had drawn in the dirt with his fingers.

Yew trees grew along the riverbank. Dar could remember his grandmother's singsong voice as she took his hand many years ago and pointed to a yew tree near their tent: "The red berry and the leaf will bring you sickness, pain, and grief." Toreg's clan had probably made the same discovery and had their own way to teach their children that the fruit and leaves of the yew tree were poisonous to eat.

Dar knew he was approaching Toreg's camp when he smelled the smoke of a campfire. His heart began to beat faster. What would happen if Toreg no longer wanted his sunstone? Or, worse, took it from him by force? Dar felt his courage draining away.

A boulder overlooked the camp and Dar peered over its top. Looking down, he saw a handful of people gathered around a fire, but where were their tents? Like Toreg, they wore fur instead of skin tunics. He could hear the faint, harsh sounds of Toreg's language.

A girl about his own age stood near the fire working with a scraper on a bearskin stretched over an upright wooden frame. He thought of his grandmother bent over her skins on the ground. He decided that she would have a standing frame like this one.

The scene before him was peaceful, but he knew these people would feel threatened if he appeared in their midst without warning. He must do something to avoid this danger and alert them as he approached the camp. Dar got down from the boulder, squared his shoulders, and entered the camp singing the yew tree song.

The people around the fire looked up with alarm. Talk and work stopped. A mother grabbed her child. Two men stood up, their hands on their knives. Everyone glared at him. Dar raised his right hand and walked closer to the fire. He laid his spear on the ground with the butt end toward them and looked around for the stranger. "Toreg?" he said with raised eyebrows.

The clan members looked surprised and several started to speak at once. Dar shook his head to let them know he could not understand them. A man spoke to the girl who had been scraping the bearskin. She was staring at Dar with a mixture of apprehension and open curiosity. After a moment of hesitation, she put down her scraper and motioned that he should follow her.

Dar picked up his spear and heard angry muttering. He replaced the spear on the ground and followed the quick-paced girl along the riverbank. After some time, he heard shouting and laughing around the next bend in the river. In a moment, he came upon the other members of the clan, divided into two boisterous work groups. Fourteen women and children were gathered on the bank cleaning salmon with long bone knives. Five men stood thigh-deep in the cold river, each holding a wooden shaft with a bone harpoon tip. The men were inside a half-circle of large rocks that had been placed in the river to form a large fish trap. Why hadn't his people thought of doing this? He would bring home another good idea to his clan.

The fish struggled to escape the rocky trap, but the men were quick, spearing the salmon and tossing them up on the bank to be gutted and scaled by the women and children. The girl pointed to one of the men who had just removed his harpoon from a writhing salmon. She cupped her hands around her mouth and shouted something that sounded to Dar like his word for father. The girl looked like Toreg; both were short and had reddish brown hair. A man glanced up and Dar shouted out his own name. Toreg waded out of the fish trap, shook the water off himself like an animal, and came toward the bank.

When he reached Dar, Toreg grinned and clapped him so hard on his shoulder that Dar could not stop himself from flinching. His manmark was still raw. Toreg spoke briefly to the girl. Before she turned and left them, she smiled at Dar. Toreg pointed to Dar's waist pouch. Dar nodded, relieved to see Toreg's interest in the sunstone. Then Dar made a snapping motion with his arm over his head. Toreg smiled and again clapped Dar on his shoulder. Dar winced and inhaled sharply. Toreg looked at Dar's fresh manmark and his eyebrows shot up. With an urgent gesture he motioned to Dar to follow him, and started off at a fast walk.

Toreg led Dar away from the river and toward the limestone cliffs. As they approached, Dar saw that the cliffs were pitted with caves and overhangs. *That's why I didn't see any tents,* Dar realized. *These people live in caves.*

Toreg stopped before one of the cave openings and beckoned Dar to follow him inside. Dar hesitated. He wished his spear were in his hand. Would he be trapped inside the cave like the salmon inside their crescent trap? Dar had to make a quick decision. He took a deep breath, put his hand on his knife, and followed Toreg into the darkness.

Inside the cave, Toreg leaned over a man who was lying between bearskin robes on a pile of goatskins. Toreg touched the man lightly on his arm. "Seelan," he said. The man sat up, his white hair tousled, his fur robe slipping from his frail upper body. Toreg looked at Dar and pointed to the old man's arm. Dar's eyes opened wide. On the arm, he saw the manmark of his own clan.

15

The Trade

Dar looked at the old man and thought of his grandmother. He had the same gray-green eyes, the same wild white hair. Dar knelt beside him and pointed to his own manmark. The old man, Seelan, caught his breath and clasped Dar in a bear hug. Then he drew back and looked at Dar. He seemed to search for the words. "Who are you?" he asked.

Dar tried to speak slowly but couldn't contain himself. "My name is Dar. You're my great-uncle! My grandmother, Mora, is your sister." Dar blurted out the next words. "And she thinks you're dead!"

Seelan shook his head. "Ah, Mora. I haven't spoken her name since I was a young man and lived among your people." Seelan pointed to his sleep robe. "Sit here beside me. We have much to tell each other."

Toreg, squatting on his heels, had been watching Dar and Seelan closely. Now he stood and spoke at some length to Seelan. He looked at Dar frequently while he talked, and at one point made the motions of one fire rock striking another. When he finished speaking, he nodded and left the cave.

"Toreg has just told me why you're here," Seelan said. "You want his spear-thrower. And he wants your wonderful stone that sparks fire. Why do I know nothing of this stone?"

"After you left the clan and before I was born," Dar said, "my grandfather traded two mammoth tusks for the sunstone."

"Ivory for fire," Seelan said. "Both things of great value."

"Why was Toreg in our territory?" Dar asked. "Was he looking for game?"

"No, he'd gone to look for some honey-colored flint he'd heard about but couldn't find," Seelan said. "He felt free to enter your territory because it wasn't marked."

Dar acknowledged this with a nod and resolved to correct this oversight. He glanced nervously around the cave. "Why are you here, Great-uncle?"

Seelan began to speak in a slow, halting voice. "I've been here since I was a young man. I had left my clan to scout for a new campsite. After days of walking, I found tracks of horse, bison, and reindeer. Something was drawing them to this area. . . ."

"The lake!" Dar interrupted.

"Yes, the lake," Seelan said. "In my excitement, I was not as watchful as I should have been. I fell into a pit trap covered with saplings and grasses that had been dug to trap woolly mammoth. Sharpened stakes had been half-buried at the bottom of the pit, and from them I suffered many wounds. I must have fainted with the pain and blood loss. When I revived, I found myself here."

"These people captured you!" Dar said.

"No," Seelan said, "they saved me."

Dar looked hard at Seelan. "Then why didn't you come home?"

Seelan threw back his robe. One of his legs ended at the ankle. A shiny layer of skin was drawn together over the stump in a rough knot. The stump had healed, but both legs were covered with scars.

"I was burning with fever and my foot had become so swollen the skin almost burst," Seelan said. "When it turned green, they took it off to save my leg . . . and probably my life."

Dar forced himself to stop staring at Seelan's legs.

Seelan's voice softened. "They cared for me like one of their own clan, Dar. I consider myself one of them and have for a long time. I have sons and grandsons whose cheeks bear their manmark." Seelan paused. "And I have made a respected place for myself here."

How could his great-uncle play a useful role in

the life of this clan? He certainly couldn't hunt or even walk unaided.

Before Seelan could continue with his story, Toreg entered the cave with his spear-thrower. He held it out to Dar, who reached into his waist pouch and took out the sunstone. Dar looked at the small yellow rock and hesitated. His fingers held the stone tightly, reluctant to let it go. Dar looked up at Toreg's expectant face and his grip loosened. He extended the sunstone to Toreg in his open hand. Toreg gently removed it from his palm. *I'll give him the flint striker, too,* Dar decided. Quickly, they made the trade, Dar clasped the spear-thrower and held it to his chest. Finally, it was his!

Dar looked at his possession. Again he was awed by the power and grace of the leaping horse carved on it. "Who can make such a thing?" he murmured.

Seelan turned and spoke briefly to Toreg in his language. Both men smiled. Seelan hit himself on his chest and turned to Dar. "I made it!"

His great-uncle, his blood relative, had carved this! Perhaps the skill was in his own blood. "It's a beautiful thing," Dar said to Seelan.

His uncle made a sweeping gesture with his hand, and Dar looked into the shadows and saw what he had missed before. Antler, bone, and mammoth tusks were stacked high against the walls.

"On clear mornings, when the sun enters my

cave, I sit near the entrance and work," Seelan said. "Because I am old, I rest in the afternoons. That's what I was doing when Toreg brought you here."

Toreg looked impatient. He spoke to Seelan, who listened and turned to Dar. "Toreg says you will need to become familiar with the use of the spear-thrower before you return home. Would you like him to get you started on how to use it tomorrow?"

Dar had watched Toreg's demonstration closely at their first meeting. "I'm not sure I need help," he said.

After his words were translated for Toreg, both men laughed. Dar flushed—he had obviously said something foolish. "Well, if Toreg has the time, tell him that would be generous of him."

Toreg seemed to understand Dar's change of mind. He nodded, touched Seelan on the arm, and left the cave.

"You must be hungry and tired," Seelan said, and his tone and expression reminded Dar of Mora. "The mother of my children died a long time ago," Seelan said. "And now my children and their children attend to my needs. Someone will bring food shortly. My teeth are old and I can eat only stews and soups, but you are welcome to share my meals and my cave."

Dar smiled. "Thank you, Great-uncle."

A short time later, a woman entered the cave

carrying a steaming bowl of food. Seelan introduced Dar to his oldest daughter, who stared at Dar even when her father was talking to her. She left and returned with a bearskin robe. The woman glanced at Seelan, as if for reassurance, then handed Dar the robe and left the cave.

After their meal, Dar watched Seelan reach for a forked wooden pole, put the crutch under his arm, and hobble to the mouth of his cave. There, using fire sticks, he started a fire in a small hearth. Dar took off his boots and gratefully slipped under the sleep robe. He looked at the little fire Seelan had built and knew it was too small to last through the night, but its warmth would help soothe him to sleep.

16

The Spear-Thrower

Sunlight was just beginning to stream into the mouth of the cave when a hand on Dar's shoulder shook him awake. It had been a long time since Dar had slept so late. He sat up with a start to find Toreg looking down at him. With a gesture, Toreg let Dar know he was to follow him, and left the cave.

Dar got up quickly and picked up his spear and new spear-thrower. He glanced at his sleeping great-uncle and then noticed the little fire still burning in the hearth at the mouth of the cave. Dar realized Seelan must have awakened throughout the night to keep it fueled.

Dar caught up with Toreg, who led him in a fast walk to an open meadow some distance from camp. They were alone. Toreg sat on a rock and with his hands indicated that Dar should begin his practice with the spear-thrower.

Dar pointed to a tree at the edge of the meadow as his target. Toreg's expression did not change.

Dar tried to remember Toreg's throwing technique. He held his spear-thrower over his right shoulder and fit the butt end of his spear to the hooked end of the antler rod. Dar tried to position his fingers, arm, and body so he could make the swift, whipping throw that had been so sure and graceful when Toreg had done it in the pine forest.

Dar took a deep breath, drew back his arm, and threw as hard as he could. The spear left his hand—so did the spear-thrower. Both fell to the ground a short distance away. Dar almost cried out in dismay. He looked quickly at Toreg to get his reaction, but Toreg's face showed nothing. Dar ran to recover his spear and spear-thrower, and resolved never again to let the antler rod leave his grasp on the throw.

Dar got back into hurtling position. He leaned back on his right leg and then quickly rocked forward on his left, putting all his body weight behind the next throw. This time, the spear-thrower stayed in his hand where it belonged, but the spear fell far short and wide of the target. Dar flushed with embarrassment.

Toreg came up to Dar's side and patted him gently on the shoulder. He dismissed Dar's target with a wave of his hand and pointed to a nearby bush. Toreg had Dar hold the spear and spear-thrower over his shoulder and then changed Dar's grip so that only Dar's thumb and forefinger held the spear on top of the spear-thrower. This left his remaining fingers free to grasp the rod near its carved handle.

Toreg barked out a word Dar thought meant *throw.* Dar threw, and the spear wobbled halfway to the target bush. Toreg again corrected Dar's grip on the spear and moved Dar's arm slowly through the hurtling cycle. Again Toreg spoke the word, issued like an order.

Toreg commanded and Dar threw for most of the long morning. When Toreg returned to his rock, Dar continued to practice under his watchful gaze. Once Toreg rose to turn Dar's body slightly. Again he got up to show Dar how to steady his spear with his left hand.

Time moved so slowly for Dar he felt he was in a dream, a dream in which he could not make his aching body do what he wanted. The sun was directly overhead when Toreg called Dar's name, pointed to his own shoulder pouch, and then to his mouth. Dar, sore and hungry, was grateful for the invitation to stop.

After Toreg's smoked salmon and pine nuts were shared and eaten, Toreg rose to leave. He nodded his encouragement to Dar and indicated that he wanted him to continue to work. Dar got to his feet, grinned, and pointed to his original target tree at the edge of the meadow. Toreg laughed, shook his head, and pointed again to the bush. He waved and left Dar to practice alone.

With Toreg gone, Dar relaxed and found his throws were better without the tension of being watched. He began to think about his throwing technique and what he had been doing, both right and wrong. Dar suddenly understood the spear-thrower: the rod acted like an extension of a hunter's arm. It enabled him to give his spear a tremendous push, forcing it to go a longer distance at a greater speed. The idea behind the spear-thrower was simple but clever. If it could be mastered, a boy could throw like a man, and a man could throw like a great hunter. He would master it and prove he had made the right decision when he traded his sunstone for the spear-thrower.

Dar continued to practice alone all afternoon. When the sun began to drop behind the limestone cliffs, he started the walk back to Seelan's cave. His muscles were stiff and painful, and the fingers of his right hand were numb. Although Dar was better at throwing than he had been in the morning, he had a long way to go before he would come close to Toreg's speed, accuracy, and power.

When Dar got back to the cave, he found Seelan awake after his afternoon rest. "You look like you're hurting, Dar."

Dar sighed as he sat down. "I'm fine. A little tired, maybe."

"My youngest daughter will come soon with the evening meal," Seelan said. "Tell me about your day of practice."

Dar rubbed his shoulder. "I had picked out a target tree far down the meadow. Toreg had me aim at a nearby bush—and I didn't hit that very often. Now I understand why you and Toreg laughed when I said I didn't need help. I did need help, a lot of it."

"What did you learn about the spear-thrower?" Seelan asked.

"That it's not magical. Now I understand why it works, even though I can't make it do what I want, yet." Dar's voice dropped. "I've spent so much time thinking the spear-thrower would solve my problem if I could only bring it home."

A young woman entered the cave carrying the evening meal, followed closely by a wide-eyed little girl. The mother smiled shyly at Dar and talked to her father briefly. The language did not sound so harsh coming from her. Dar smiled at them both, and the child was giggling by the time she and her mother left.

Seelan gave Dar a small bowl with a handle and pointed to the stewpot. "What problem?"

Dar's expression turned serious—he was sorry he'd spoken about his problem. He thought what he was about to say would sound foolish, but Seelan was so much like his grandmother that he felt safe.

"I'm small. I thought all I had to do was fit my spear to my spear-thrower and it would make me big. It looked so easy when Toreg did it."

"You'll learn, Dar," Seelan said. "Remember, you're getting more out of the trade than you thought you would. You not only have the spear-thrower but a good teacher as well. And you've no doubt noticed that Toreg is also short?"

Dar smiled. "Yes, I've noticed. And Toreg is a good teacher. He never acts like I'm hopeless."

"Because you're not," Seelan said. "Everybody must go through a beginner's phase to learn anything difficult. Even Toreg. Dar, eat your stew and go to sleep. You need some healing time."

Seelan got out his fire sticks, and Dar watched carefully as his great-uncle started the night fire at the mouth of the cave. "While I'm with you," Dar said, "I will get up to keep the fire burning through the night."

17

The Dagger-Tooth Cat

Throughout his second night with Seelan, Dar arose at regular intervals to fuel the night fire. Twice he saw the eyes of animals gleaming at him from beyond the cave entrance. When Dar awoke in the morning, Seelan was seated in the sunlit mouth of the cave. He had thrown a leather hide over his lap and was working on a piece of ivory. Dar got up to join him.

"Thank you for keeping the night fire burning," Seelan said to him. "Without a fire, we might be sharing this cave with a hibernating bear or a wolf mother and her cubs."

Dar thought of the gleaming eyes and had a new appreciation for his own clan's skin tents, which did not attract cave-dwelling animals.

Dar squatted to watch his great-uncle. Seelan cut two deep, circular grooves around the ivory piece, three fingers apart, with a flint chisel of a kind Dar had never seen before. Its beveled point dug deep into the ivory without shattering it.

"That's mammoth tusk, isn't it?" Dar asked. "What are you making?"

"It's a small piece of a tusk that was once taller than you are," Seelan answered. "I'm making Mora a bracelet for you to take home to her."

Dar sat down close to Seelan. His great-uncle picked up a mallet of antler and struck the ivory at the two places weakened by the grooves. The ivory broke cleanly, leaving a hollow circle in Seelan's hands. Then he began to work on the circle using the side edge of his chisel.

Dar never took his eyes off Seelan's hands. "Great-uncle, your old clan has been without you for many, many seasons. You and your carving skills would have added so much to our lives."

Seelan shook his head regretfully. "My old clan didn't value my skills. My father told me carving was a waste of time. To hunt well was what a man was supposed to do."

"Nothing has changed," Dar said. "I tried to teach myself to carve, but my uncle didn't understand my interest. In fact, it made him angry. He told me I had more important things to learn."

"Are you talking about Mora's son, Kenok?" Seelan asked. Dar nodded. "He was a little boy when I left," Seelan continued, "and my sister was carrying her second child."

"That second child became my father," Dar said,

then stopped speaking. Seelan waited for him to continue and his quiet interest again reminded Dar of his grandmother. "My father's dead," he said.

Seelan put down his chisel. "I'm sorry, Dar."

"He was killed by a strange animal just before I was born," Dar continued.

"Tell me what was strange about the animal," Seelan said.

"I was told it was like a lion but with two huge teeth that hung down over its lower jaw," Dar said. "No one had ever seen or heard of such an animal. Kenok was with my father when he was killed, and Uncle thinks it was a spirit creature sent to test him."

"That was no spirit creature," Seelan said. "I used to hear the old men of this clan talk about such an animal. They told me hunters used to kill one occasionally, and sometimes hunters were killed by them. It's called a dagger-tooth cat. They hold down their prey with their strong forelimbs, then rip it open with those dagger teeth. No one has seen one since I've been here, but people still tell stories about them, especially during our dances and ceremonies."

Dar tried to picture the cat in his mind.

Seelan's voice became low and full of feeling. "Kenok must have suffered . . . is probably still suffering."

Dar thought of Kenok's quick anger. "Why is he still suffering?"

"Because he lives thinking he failed the spirit test," Seelan answered, "and this failure led to the death of his brother."

Dar had lived with his uncle's black moods as long as he could remember, and he often felt he was the cause of them. He had never considered there might be another reason for Kenok's temperament that had nothing to do with him.

Seelan picked up his chisel and the circle of ivory and held them up. "Dar, this interests you. I know you thought you would stay here only for a night or two. But stay longer and I'll begin to teach you how to work on bone, antler, and ivory. They're better than wood or flint for making weapons. You need special flint chisels for the work, but I'll help you make these, too. We'll spend the mornings together and you can practice with the spear-thrower in the afternoons while I rest."

Dar's face lit up, but he hesitated before answering.

Seelan smiled. "It won't be all work," he said. "Toreg tells me that a small herd of musk oxen have been sighted moving down from their winter pasture to look for the new spring grasses. When they enter the far end of the valley, Toreg and some others will hunt them. He wants you to go along."

The invitation jolted Dar. "This will be my first real hunt and I'll be using the spear-thrower." Dar's voice came out in a whisper. "I'm afraid of failing in front of Toreg and the other hunters."

"Would you rather take a chance of failing in front of Kenok at home?"

"No!" Dar burst out, and Seelan laughed at the force of his answer. Dar tried to revive his sinking confidence. "I'll be the only hunter in my clan to have a spear-thrower."

"Dar, what do you think is going to happen when you get home and the men see your spear-thrower and find out what it can do?" Seelan asked.

The answer to Seelan's question was obvious and Dar's shoulders slumped. Why hadn't he thought of this before? Dar spoke in a subdued voice. "They'll all want one."

"That's right," Seelan said.

Dar tried hard to recover from this blow. "Well, I could be the person who makes spear-throwers for the other hunters in my clan. Will you teach me how to make them, with a carved animal on their handles?"

"Spear-throwers like yours aren't easy to make," Seelan said. "Remember what you learned yesterday? First target the bush, not the tree. When you return to your clan, start making some spear-throwers out of wood. When you get good at this, switch to antler. When you feel you really understand what you're doing, then start carving animals on them."

"I have a lot to learn from you and Toreg," Dar said. "I will stay here a little while longer, Great-uncle."

18

Bone, Antler, and Ivory

When Dar woke up the next morning, Seelan was already at work. Impressed by the old man's energy, Dar got up quickly to join him.

Seelan stopped what he was doing to greet him. "Dar, why don't you start by carving something your grandmother could use to make her life easier? Does she have any ivory or bone needles?"

"No, just wooden ones," Dar answered. "I've grown up listening to her outbursts when they break in her hand while she's at work on a piece of skin."

Seelan smiled. "That sounds like the sister I remember. Here's a piece of ivory left over from my bracelet. Sit beside me and throw this hide over your lap for protection."

Dar took the hide and sat down. "I don't know how to begin. I've never worked on ivory before."

"You'll learn," Seelan said. "Ivory is good to start with. It's not as brittle as bone or antler, and it takes a polish well." He picked up his flint chisel and scratched an outline of a small needle on the ivory. "You're going to take the chisel, follow my scratch marks, and cut deep, angled grooves that meet below the surface of the ivory. Go slowly until you have a feel for what you're doing."

Dar worked cautiously, trying to trace Seelan's marks exactly. He cut deeper into the material with each chisel stroke. Finally Seelan said, "Do you think your needle has been separated from the rest of the ivory?"

Worried, Dar made several more careful strokes in the grooves.

"Now watch," Seelan said, taking Dar's piece from him. When Seelan pressed hard on the wide end of the needle, the entire needle popped up from the ivory. "You did a good job, Dar. The needle wouldn't have come out if your grooves hadn't been deep and accurate."

Dar grinned. "What about the eye of the needle?"

"In good time," Seelan answered. "Thin down the wide end of the needle with this sandstone. When you think it's thin enough, take this little flint awl and bore a hole in it. Be careful, it's a delicate job."

Dar rubbed the wide end of the needle with the sandstone until he thought it thin enough to start drilling the eye. Working first on one side and then the other, he quickly bored a clean hole just where he wanted it. He held the needle up for Seelan's approval.

"Fine so far, but you're not quite finished," Seelan said. "Use this scraper to make the needle smooth and round. And when you've done that, rub it back and forth on the sandstone to sharpen the point and polish it."

The needle gradually changed as Dar worked on it, becoming round and smooth and sharp at the tip. He looked up and smiled. "Now I know how to make a needle!"

"You've learned far more than that," Seelan said. "You'll use almost the same method for whatever you want to make. What would you like to do now?"

"I'd like to make a spearpoint out of antler, like Toreg's," Dar said. "I know that Bowan, the boy I was initiated with, will want one."

"That's a generous idea, Dar," Seelan said. "He must be a close friend."

Dar was embarrassed; he had been misunderstood. "I didn't mean I was going to make one for him, just that he'll be envious of mine." Seelan said nothing. "We've never been close," Dar said.

Seelan shook his head. "It must have been lonely growing up without the friendship of the only boy in your clan your own age. Why isn't he your friend?" Seelan asked.

"He's always looked down on me," Dar answered. "Bowan is bigger than I am—and usually braver."

"Well, you're changing," Seelan said. "It took

courage to come here. Are you sure the height of a person really matters in a friendship?"

Dar sat still, thinking about Seelan's question.

Seelan stretched to pick up an antler lying in a nearby pot of water. "I keep some antler soaking to soften it. Dar, get started on your spearpoint. Scratch its shape on the surface of this antler. Then cut grooves into the scratch marks deep enough to reach the soft center. When you're sure you've gone deep enough, gently pry out your spearpoint."

Dar still worked slowly but with more confidence. When he pried the spearpoint from the antler, it wasn't as smooth as he would have liked, but it was in one piece.

Seelan looked up and nodded his encouragement. "You've told me what bothers you about Bowan. Is there anything about him you like?"

Dar answered quickly and easily. "He's full of energy and he knows a lot. I don't like it, but he's better at flint work than I am."

"He doesn't sound like a bad person," Seelan said. "Are you sure he looks down on you? Maybe the problem has been that you've looked up to him and—as you said—you haven't liked that."

Dar could feel his face flush. He turned to pick up the flint scraper and began to smooth down the spearpoint. He was grateful to have work to do as he thought about Bowan and what Seelan was telling him. Dar remembered when Bowan had refused to enter the sacred cave first, showing his fear to Dar for the first time. Dar had been surprised at his own reaction to this. Instead of satisfaction, Dar had felt only sympathy for Bowan. And this feeling had lasted throughout the initiation ceremony.

Dar sharpened his weapon. Seelan was right, it had been lonely growing up without a close friend. When he finished the spearpoint, he held it up. "I'm going to give this to Bowan—and start making antler points for all the hunters when I get home."

Seelan looked up and smiled, then returned to etching an elaborate design on the creamy surface of the bracelet.

"Grandmother will love your gift," Dar said, and was swept by a wave of affection for both Mora and Seelan. "I can't wait to tell her about you, your life here, your carving. There's nothing like this bracelet in our clan."

"Maybe someday there will be other such pieces," Seelan said. "Dar, why do you want to be a carver?"

Dar had never asked himself why he wanted to carve and had to think before answering. "I used to have the job of lighting the morning fire. I carved little animals on scraps of wood before the others were up. It was my favorite time of day. It was quiet, I felt free and in charge. And even if my work wasn't very good, the ideas and decisions were mine."

"I know these feelings well," Seelan said. "But it sounds like the carving stopped when the morning fire was no longer your job."

"Yes, I thought I'd have to give up carving after my initiation when I became a man, a hunter. And when I saw Toreg's spear-thrower, I thought I could never make anything like that." Dar smiled at Seelan. "You've made me change my mind."

"I'm glad I have, Dar," Seelan said. "I like making tools and weapons, but it's been more important to me to try to capture the spirit of an animal in my carving." He shrugged. "Of course, I don't always succeed."

Dar's voice rose. "But the leaping horse looks so alive!"

"In a lifetime of carving, Dar, there have been both failures and successes," Seelan said. "But it's been a good life."

Dar nodded, almost to himself. A good life.

19

Circle of Horns

Dar had never been so busy. In the mornings, under Seelan's guidance, he worked on bone, antler, and ivory with five different kinds of flint chisels that Seelan had helped him make. Dar found Seelan's flint-work instructions similar to Kenok's attempts to teach him, but he learned easily from his great-uncle.

"You'll go home with the tools you need to cut, pierce, gouge, smooth, polish, and engrave," Seelan told him. "Experiment with your chisels. You'll find which works best for the job."

In the afternoons, Dar practiced with his spear-thrower, usually watched by the children of the clan. They gathered at the edge of the meadow, pointing, laughing, and offering advice that Dar could not understand. When Toreg came by every day to judge Dar's progress, he shooed the children away. When he left, they returned.

Dar was slowly improving. He hit the target bush more often, and his body no longer ached. He thought his right arm was more muscular than it used to be. Dar hoped his father's bracelet would fit him now.

Toreg's visits to the meadow grew more infrequent, but he was there when Dar hit the target three times in a row. On the fourth successful throw, Toreg let out a yelp of approval and pointed to Dar's original target, the tree. He left Dar alone to work.

Dar tried to hit the tree trunk for one entire afternoon but missed every time. He was glad Toreg wasn't there to see his failures, although the children were. They seemed more sympathetic to his efforts now and there was less laughter.

The next day, Dar's spear hit the target tree for the first time, and the children's cheers rang out. After that, the spear sank into the trunk with increasing regularity. Dar thought of the coming hunt. "I'm ready," he said out loud, but his mouth was dry.

Early the next morning, just after Seelan and Dar had moved to their work area, Toreg appeared. He spoke to Seelan, pointed to Dar, and left. "Musk oxen have been seen at the far end of the valley," Seelan translated for Dar. "A hunting party is gathering in your practice meadow. They'll be moving out as soon as you join them."

Dar ran back inside the cave to get his knife,

spear, and spear-thrower and returned to Seelan. "What if my spear throw is bad or I get in the way of the others?" Dar said. He thought of sharp horns and Kenok's bloody wounds. He didn't tell Seelan he was afraid of getting hurt or killed.

"Dar, you're bound to learn something no matter what happens," Seelan said. "Toreg's a fine hunter. Watch what he does and try to figure out why he does it. And look at the musk oxen closely. You might want to carve one someday."

Dar's spirits lifted. He waved good-bye and hurried to the meadow. Toreg and five other hunters were waiting for him. They ranged in age from a young man with a fresh manmark on his cheek to a gray-haired hunter much older than Toreg. All were carrying at least two spears, and their spear-throwers were tucked into their belts. Dar quickly secured his in the same way.

He was puzzled by the folded deer hides Toreg and two other men carried over their shoulders. Dar tried to guess their purpose, as Seelan had suggested, but was unable to do so.

Clearly in charge, Toreg gave a signal and the men started forward at a ground-covering lope. They talked as they moved, and Dar wished he could join their conversation or at least understand it. The pace was maintained until the valley widened and they entered a broader meadow filled with waving green grasses. The hunters stopped talking and hurried to waist-high bushes and sank behind them.

Toreg had the youngest hunter come to his side. The young man put down his hunting gear and, with Toreg's help, stood on Toreg's shoulders. He scanned the meadow, pointed, and jumped to the ground—the musk oxen had been sighted. The men smiled and Dar sensed their rising excitement. His own breathing became more rapid and his heart beat faster.

Toreg separated the hunters into two groups. Three men were to go to the left of the herd and two men to the right. Toreg indicated that Dar was to stay behind with him. The hunters, keeping the wind in their faces, crouched and crawled through the tall grass toward the herd.

Dar strained to see the animals through the bushes. One large bull, five adult females, three calves, and four half-grown adults were grazing in the meadow. The thick-set bodies of the musk oxen were covered with coarse hair that hung to the ground. Dar studied them carefully. Their dangerous horns grew out of a heavy bony headband that covered their foreheads. The adult animals looked well able to defend themselves and their young against attack. One toss of a massive head could rip a wolf or a man wide open.

The bull caught the scent of the hunters, snorted, and shook his head in warning. Toreg, with a half-smile on his face, stood motionless at Dar's side while the other hunters got into position closer to the herd. Dar admired Toreg's confidence, but shouldn't he give the signal to start the attack?

Instead, Toreg did something Dar did not expect. He stepped forward toward the watchful animals, unfolded his leather hide, and raised it over his head. He yelled as he flapped it back and forth. Then hides were raised in the two other groups, and now all the men started to yell. But still no spear-thrower was lifted, no spear attached.

After a moment of milling confusion, the mature musk oxen formed a tight circle around the young adults and calves. With lowered heads facing outward, they pawed the ground and bellowed at the hunters. Dar heard the younger animals bleating within the circle of angry adults.

And now Toreg dropped his hide, raised his spear for the others to see, then attached it to his spear-thrower. Trembling with excitement, Dar got his own spear-thrower and spear into place. He and Toreg joined the other hunters as they closed in and formed a wide circle of men around the tight circle of horns. They moved in just close enough for their spears to strike the musk oxen.

The work of killing began, and the shouts of the

hunters mingled with the bellowing of the animals. Dar took aim and threw with all his strength. His spear arced and flew into the huddle of musk oxen and disappeared in the clouds of dust stirred up by the jittery herd.

After all the spears were thrown, the hunters watched as two adult females, both wounded and bawling with rage and pain, left the circle. They were followed by the young adults and calves. The animals headed back toward their winter home above the valley floor. Four musk oxen remained in their stubborn circle, dead.

Dar ran up to the circle with the other hunters to examine the carcasses and retrieve the spears. Dar saw his own spear deep in the side of a large female and shouted in triumph. His success had to be shared with another hunter whose spear was also embedded in the same musk ox. At least his own throw had found its mark and had contributed to the kill.

Toreg clapped Dar on his back and then spoke to the youngest hunter, who turned and left the group at a fast trot. Dar guessed he had been sent back to camp to tell the others to come help with the butchering and carrying. Nothing would be wasted. Meat, sinew, hides, and horn would all be taken back to camp before sundown. Otherwise, scavenging animals would find the kill and deprive the hunters of their success.

Dar got out his knife to join in the work of butchering and soon, like the others, was covered with fat, hair, and blood. With the fierce intensity of the hunt gone, the hunters talked and laughed as they worked.

Dar was flooded with a sense of pride and relief. And he was filled with a deep respect for the musk oxen. The animals had put up a courageous fight to guard their young within the circle. But it was a formation designed to protect them from wolf and lion, not the spears and spear-throwers of the hunters. Their ancient defense strategy had led to their slaughter.

Someday Dar would carve an angry bull, its head lowered against all enemies, protective and defiant. Dar looked at the bloody, dismembered musk oxen piled around him. The bull he carved would live forever.

20

▷

An Invitation

◁

Dar's muscles ached from the butchering, and he was tired from the long walk back to Seelan's cave, but he was so happy he hardly noticed.

Seelan, eating his evening meal, looked up as Dar entered. "I've heard it was a good hunt, and I can tell by your face that you did well."

Dar put down his gear. "I felt like a hunter, like a man."

"You worked hard for it." Seelan pushed a bowl of fragrant stew toward Dar. "Adulthood doesn't come with the initiation. The ceremony is only a signal that you're ready to begin to earn it. That's what you've been doing, Dar."

"I'm not sure I understood that before," Dar said. Although hungry, he ignored the food in front of him. "Great-uncle, I should start for home tomorrow."

Seelan stopped eating and put aside his bowl. "Dar, I've been thinking. You could stay here with us. I like having you here and so does Toreg. He has no sons of his own. If you stay, I will teach you all I know about carving. Someday you would be a master carver, able to take my place when I'm gone."

Dar was unprepared for this invitation and was silent for a moment. Finally he said, "Part of me wants to stay. I've been happy here with you and Toreg. I know I want to become a master carver. But I can't give you my answer now, Great-uncle. I will make up my mind by morning."

Dar ate his meal and made the night fire. He lay between his fur robes, but was restless with indecision. *If I stay,* Dar said to himself, *Seelan and Toreg would be a part of my life and I'd be free of Kenok forever.*

Dar got up throughout the night to refuel the fire. Just before dawn, he lay awake and struggled to understand what a great snowy owl had said to him in a dream. Dar sat up on his bearskin and found Seelan awake, looking at him.

"Great-uncle," Dar said, "I can't stay here."

Seelan rolled over on his side and rested his head on his hand. "Why not?"

"I had a dream last night about a white owl with shimmering feathers. It was trying to tell me something important, but its voice sounded like the flute at my initiation ceremony. Only after I woke up and thought about it did I understand its message."

"What was its message?" Seelan asked.

"The owl was our shaman in his white ceremonial

cape," Dar answered. "At our initiation, after our manmarks had been cut, the shaman held his great knife over his head and spoke directly to Bowan and me. He told us we would come into our manhood to serve the clan, not ourselves. I think that's what the owl's flute song was telling me in my dream."

Seelan nodded, but his face was sad.

Dar went on. "When I was younger, I thought being a man meant I would be free, that no one would be able to tell me what to do."

Seelan shifted on his robe. "All young boys have those dreams. I know I did."

Dar continued. "I thought because I came here to get the spear-thrower, I would have the only one in my clan, forever. It never occurred to me that every hunter would want one—and should have one. My grandfather must have found out the same thing after he brought the first sunstone into our clan long ago. . . . Everyone has one now."

Seelan's voice was low. "So you feel you must go home to bring the idea of the spear-thrower to the hunters of your clan?"

"Yes, but I have responsibilities to my people beyond the spear-thrower, particularly to my grandmother," Dar said. "I owe her a great debt which I haven't begun to repay. She's cared for me since my mother's death shortly after I was born."

"I didn't know this, Dar," Seelan said, then was

silent. Finally, he shook his head and faced Dar. "You've understood your dream shaman well. It was selfish of me to try to persuade you to stay. How could I have asked you to leave Mora? Aside from any special debt you owe her, she needs you. I, above all people, should know that old people must depend upon their families. Dar, your answer was better than my question." Seelan hesitated. "I would have returned, too, had I been able."

Dar welcomed these words. He wanted to know that Seelan felt a bond with his old clan. And it made Dar more secure in his own decision to go home.

Dar thought longingly of Seelan's offer to continue to teach him. "About the carving—"

Seelan interrupted. "I taught myself to carve. You've had a good beginning. Dar, you are a carver in your heart. Your hands will follow its lead."

Dar swallowed hard. Seelan had given him a great gift: confidence in his ability to learn on his own.

While Dar was making preparations for his journey home, Toreg came into the cave and solemnly handed Dar his own fire sticks. Dar looked into Toreg's face and reached out to embrace him. Toreg hugged him back and gently put his hand on Dar's manmark. Then Toreg turned away, spoke briefly to Seelan, and quickly left the cave.

"Toreg says you have grown into your manmark," Seelan said with a catch in his voice.

"Please thank Toreg for all his help and patience," Dar said to Seelan. "Tell him our clans should not be so distant from each other. I hope he will come again to our territory and be welcomed by my clan." Dar thought a moment. Toreg had given him a great deal; he would give something in return. "Great-uncle, I know all your people will want sunstones after seeing how well they work. Tell Toreg to look for small yellow rocks in the river or on its banks where the nearby mountains rise most steeply out of the valley floor. He must search for the rocks on a sunny day because, if there are sunstones, they will shimmer in the sunlight."

"That's important to know, Dar; I will tell him," Seelan said. "You and Toreg have made a good trade. Both clans will gain from it." Dar welcomed the words. He was sure he would not hear them from Kenok.

Seelan reached into a basket and got out the ivory bracelet. It was covered with a complicated spiral design that had no beginning or end. "Tell Mora she's the one I've missed the most." Seelan handed Dar the bracelet. "I will miss you, too, Dar."

Dar knelt to embrace Seelan. "Thank you, Great-uncle, for everything you have done for me." Dar put the bracelet into his empty waist pouch and started to leave Seelan's cave. He stopped and turned. "You will live within me all of my life."

21

In the Pine Forest

Dar moved with the fast lope of the musk ox hunters as he left the valley and started for home. He felt differently about himself; he was not the same person who had entered Toreg's camp twelve days ago. He knew he had learned a great deal there, but at the same time he felt his learning had just begun. That was it—he had made a beginning.

Dar remembered singing the yew tree song on first entering the camp. He realized he had sung the song not only to warn the new clan of his presence, but to give himself courage. The trip home would be long and lonely. He might have to sing the song again before he returned to his own clan.

Along the way, Dar found enough edible plants to keep him fed, and he caught an occasional rabbit; the spear-thrower remained in his shoulder pouch. When he came to Bone Lake, he took the long way around. His journey had almost ended there, but he had learned some useful things from the experience. He slept on piles of leaves at night and built windbreaks when cold winds blew.

Dar thought of what Seelan had said about observing the musk oxen, and he began to look closely at the smaller animals around him. How could he carve the prickled fur of a hedgehog, how far apart were a rabbit's eyes, how big was a beaver's tail in proportion to its body? He carved them all in his mind.

After nine days of hard walking, Dar entered the pine forest as the sun was going down. In the fading light, he took his knife and carved his clan's manmark on three of the pine trunks. Seelan had told him Toreg would not have come into his clan's territory if these marks had been there before. Dar was glad the forest had been unmarked, and that Toreg had entered it—and Dar's life.

Dar skinned the rabbit he had caught earlier and spitted it over a small fire. As night fell, he relaxed in the territory of his own clan and waited for his meal to cook in the sputtering flames.

His tranquil mood did not last long. He was startled to hear footsteps moments before a large man loomed above him and Kenok's angry voice rang out. "Where have you been? Your grandmother thinks you're dead!"

Dar rose to face his uncle. "I'm very much alive," he said in a resolute voice.

Kenok stepped close to Dar. "I said, where have you been?"

Dar spoke slowly, emphasizing every word. "I went to the stranger's camp to trade my sunstone for his spear-thrower."

Kenok glared at him. "How could you do such a stupid thing? And how could you leave without telling me? Mora knew where you went, didn't she?"

"Yes, Grandmother knew, but don't blame her. I asked her not to tell anyone," Dar said, his voice rising. "I'm an adult now. I don't need your permission any longer."

Kenok's eyes were hard. "It's not a question of asking for permission. You should have told me where you were going. You knew I wouldn't like your plan, but I could not have forbidden it. You say you're an adult, but you kept your trip a secret like a child."

Dar knew from the feeling in the pit of his stomach that Kenok was right. But he was too angry to admit it now. Fists clenched, they stood opposite each other in the forest clearing.

Kenok bit off his words. "You don't seem to understand that my job has been to prepare you to be a man."

Dar's eyes locked with Kenok's. "That's what fathers do, and you aren't my father."

"You're right, I'm not your father." Kenok spoke

with fury and stepped closer to Dar. "And you're not my son. You've resented me for trying to teach you what you must know. You've refused to learn from me."

"You haven't acted like a father to me." Dar was embarrassed to find his voice choking up. "You've never even liked me."

"What's that got to do with it?" Kenok shot back. "You've been my responsibility, one I didn't want. But I've kept you safe. You've never been hungry, never been without clothes or shelter."

Dar felt his heart pounding. "Grandmother has done this for me. She makes the meals I eat, the clothes I wear. She even made the tent we live in."

Kenok slowly shook his head. "You have a wise and strong grandmother, but she also has needs. I'm her only living son and I have commitments to you both. Don't you see, Dar? Mora made the tent; I provided the skins."

Dar heard a new tone in Kenok's voice and his own voice softened. "Perhaps you're right. You've cared for me for years . . . in place of my father."

Kenok stepped back and unclenched his fists. "I loved your father, Dar. He was more than a brother to me. He was my deepest friend. And I failed him, I failed the test. I could not save him from the spirit cat."

Dar moved close to Kenok. "You didn't fail the

spirit test. There was no test. The animal that killed my father was real!"

Kenok looked startled. "What are you talking about? Who told you that?"

"Grandmother's brother, Seelan!" Dar said.

Kenok's eyes opened wide as if he could not take in all this new information. "Seelan? Seelan there? Not dead?" The words came out like drumbeats.

"No." Dar echoed the rhythm of his uncle's words. "Alive. Crippled. A carver—and respected for it."

With the anger drained out of them, Dar and Kenok sat on the ground by the fire. Kenok leaned forward to listen as Dar told him the story of Seelan.

"A remarkable old man," Kenok said when Dar stopped speaking. Kenok took a deep breath. "Now, tell me what Seelan said about the spirit creature."

"Uncle, it's not a spirit creature," Dar said. "Their clan calls it a dagger-tooth cat. Nobody has seen one since Seelan's been there, but the old hunters used to talk about the cat to Seelan. It's still part of the clan's legends and ceremonies."

Kenok frowned. "Perhaps Seelan is right and the animal is of this world. Perhaps not. . . ." Kenok turned away from the subject abruptly. "Tell me about the stranger and his clan."

Dar talked about Toreg and the ways of his people, and Kenok heard the story with intense interest. He asked so many questions that Dar went on to tell him about the spear-thrower, Toreg's skill, and his own struggle to master the antler rod.

Dar had never spoken so freely or at such length to his uncle. When he finished, Kenok said, "Let me see the spear-thrower you went so far to get."

Dar took the rod out of his shoulder pouch and handed it to Kenok. "Seelan made this."

Kenok held the spear-thrower close to the light of the fire and turned it over and over in his hands. "This is beautiful, Dar."

"Seelan got me started working with bone, antler, and ivory," Dar said. "And he helped me make flint carving tools to take home. I watched him make a wonderful ivory bracelet for Grandmother." Dar took it out of his waist pouch, handed it to Kenok, and took back the spear-thrower. As they talked, Kenok traced the design on the bracelet with his fingertips.

"Seelan taught me to think like a carver," Dar said. He paused and then spoke in an assured voice he did not know he possessed. "That's what I'm going to be."

Kenok shifted his position, and his voice regained its edge. "What about hunting?"

"I'll do that, too. A man must hunt," Dar said.

Kenok looked relieved. Dar paused before continu-ing. "But I did consider staying with Seelan and his clan."

Kenok raised his eyebrows. "*His* clan?"

"Yes, they are his people now. His sons and grandsons all bear that clan's manmark on their cheeks."

Kenok grew thoughtful. "You liked it there, Dar. Seelan and Toreg were good to you. What made you decide to return?"

"Yes, they were good to me," Dar said. "But I had a choice and Seelan didn't. He couldn't walk home. I thought about the sons I may have some-day—and their sons. I want them all to carry our manmark on their arms."

Kenok looked intently at Dar. "Your father speaks through you."

Kenok had never linked him to his father before, and Dar felt tears in his eyes. In the low, flickering light, Dar thought Kenok's eyes were also wet.

Dar remembered the rabbit and removed it from the fire. He took out his knife and cut the over-cooked meat into two pieces. "Share my meal. We'll be home by tomorrow noon, and the food will be better there."

Kenok smiled. "I hope so." He returned the bracelet to Dar and reached for his charred portion of rabbit. They ate in comfortable silence until

Kenok tossed his last bone into the fire. "Tomorrow, I want you to show me how the spear-thrower works—if it works."

Dar nodded and found himself nervously humming the yew tree song under his breath. *Courage.*

Kenok winced with pain as he stretched out beside the fire to sleep. Dar started to question him about his wound, but Kenok held up his hand to silence him."No more talk, Dar. We need to sleep."

22

The Challenge

◁

Dar was the first to get up the next morning. An early ray of sunlight struck a large rock and, to Dar's surprise, revealed a healing plant half-hidden behind it. This lucky find would please his grandmother.

Dar started to pull off its leaves and purple flowers, but stopped. He turned to Kenok, who was slowly getting up. "I'm going to take home the whole plant, roots and all," Dar said. "Grandmother can put it back in the ground near the river." He began to dig up the plant and grinned. "Perhaps, like Seelan, it will become a useful and respected member of its new clan."

Kenok laughed. "I would welcome it if it decides to live among us." His face grew serious. "Dar, I never thanked you for going up that rocky ledge to get the healing plants after I was gored. You helped save my life."

"The spirits wanted you to live, Uncle, but I see you're still in pain."

"My shoulder has healed but my leg still hurts. It will mend soon," Kenok said. "Now, Dar, give me a demonstration of what your spear-thrower can do."

"We'll do it together," Dar said and pointed to a tree far from where they stood. "See if you can reach that tree trunk with your spear."

Kenok shook his head. "I'm not sure I can." He readied his spear and threw with all his strength. The spear fell short. Kenok's tone was challenging. "Your turn."

Dar took out his spear-thrower and got into throwing position. He was less tense than he expected to be. He attached his spear to the spear-thrower and hurled the spear in one quick, flowing motion. It flew toward the target, fast and sure, and struck the trunk and stayed there, quivering.

Dar stood proudly and waited for Kenok to speak.

Kenok stared at the tree in amazement, then took the spear-thrower from Dar and turned it in his hands. "All right, Dar, I see that it works." Kenok was silent for a moment. "If I'd had a spear-thrower when I was going after that bison, maybe I wouldn't have needed to get so close to make my throw." Kenok broke off again, then finally said, "Will you make me one?"

"Gladly, Uncle, but it will have to be a simple

one, made of wood," Dar said. "When I become more skillful, I'll make you one of antler. Then you can choose the animal you want me to carve on it. Your spear-thrower won't be as beautiful as one carved by Seelan, but it will be as fine as I can make it."

Kenok smiled his thanks and began to collect his belongings. Dar left him to retrieve the spears. A quick movement in the distance made Dar look up to the craggy foothills beyond the pine forest. Perched on an overhang, beyond the reach of spear and spear-thrower, a large cat stretched its long legs and powerful body in the morning sunlight. Dar squinted into the sun, and his heart seemed to stop. The cat's teeth jutted down over its lower jaw like daggers.

Dar ran back to Kenok and silently started to lead him to a spot where he could also see the cat.

Kenok resisted Dar's pull on his arm. "Where are you taking me? Why are you so excited?"

Dar pointed to the overhang.

Kenok looked up and grew very still. "The spirit creature has come again," he murmured.

"No," Dar said. "A dagger-tooth cat is sunning itself on a ledge." But Kenok gave no sign he'd heard Dar. "Uncle, put down the burden of the spirit test. My father's death was not your fault. You tried to protect him from an animal just like the one we see. If there *had* been a spirit test, why would you have been saved?" Dar spoke slowly in a low voice. "I'm glad you lived."

The cat seemed to hear them and turned its head sharply in their direction. It snarled, jumped to a higher ledge, and then was gone.

Kenok stood staring at the empty ledge and was quiet for a long time. "Perhaps you're right, Nephew," he finally said, and turned to face Dar. "Someday, when you're able to make me a rod of antler, will you carve a dagger-tooth cat on it?"

"Of course," Dar answered. "And no one else will have such a spear-thrower."

When they returned to their overnight campsite, Dar was surprised to see the amount of gear his uncle had brought to the pine forest. Kenok's three pouches bulged and he had an extra spear. Dar had noticed none of this in last night's darkness.

"Why did you bring so much with you just to empty the traps?" Dar asked. "You look like you have enough supplies for a long journey."

"I was setting out on a long journey—I was coming to look for you," Kenok said. "I had planned to go as far as the lake Mora talks about."

Dar's eyes opened wide. "But you're still recovering from your accident."

"Dar, your grandmother is sick with worry over you. Everyone is worried." Kenok paused. "I was worried."

Dar put his hand on Kenok's shoulder. "Thank you, Uncle, for starting on such a trip. I'm glad we discovered each other here in the pine forest."

Dar started to gather up his belongings. Kenok put out the last embers of the fire and picked up his gear. He walked away with an uneven gait, leaning on one of his spears for support.

Dar easily caught up with him, and the two men walked out of the pine forest, headed for home.

Afterword

The story of *Dar and the Spear-Thrower* takes place during the Magdalenian period, which flourished in France between twenty thousand and eleven thousand years ago. Dar was quick to appreciate the value of the spear-thrower, a Magdalenian invention. This device was later replaced by a weapon even more effective and deadly, the bow and arrow.

The "sunstone" that Dar's clan used to start their fires was iron pyrite, a yellow rock with a brilliant luster. The Magdalenians discovered that this hard-to-find mineral, when struck with flint, would produce sparks hot enough to ignite tinder.

During the period of this story, woolly rhinoceros and mammoth, musk ox, horse, bison, and lion all inhabited the region where Dar lived. Gradually, many animals disappeared from western Europe. Some scientists believe the European musk ox was wiped out by hunters who knew how to take advantage of their "circle of horns" formation.

Because of inadequate fossil material, it is difficult for scientists to be certain of the extinction date
of the sabertooth cat in Europe. Sabertooth fossils
dating to Dar's time have been found in England,
but not in France. The Lesser Scimitar was the last
of the sabertooth cats still living in Europe before
total extinction would claim the entire species. This
is the dagger-tooth cat of the story—a rare creature
used to suggest the magical power of a mysterious
animal.

The Magdalenian people produced the most
magnificent artwork of the Stone Age. Seelan's
spear-thrower with its leaping horse is modeled
after an actual spear-thrower that survives in the
Musée des Antiquités Nationales near Paris. The
paintings Dar sees in the sacred cave are those
found on the walls and ceilings of Lascaux, the
great "temple cave" in southern France. Dar's
dream of the animal with "the legs of a lion and
the belly of a pregnant mare" describes a creature
painted on the walls of Lascaux. The dance that
ends Dar's initiation ceremony is based on foot-
prints found on the floor of another painted cave in
that region.

The references in the book to the fat-fuel lamp,
the ivory needle and bracelet, the elegant flint
ceremonial knife, the bone flute, and the antler

harpoons and spearpoints are also based on arti-
facts that can be seen in museums today.

When the Ice Age came to an end in Europe, the
hunting bands either followed the cold-adapted
animal herds north, or stayed to invent another way
of securing food for themselves, one dependent on
planting and reaping instead of hunting and gathering. People began to live close to the fields they
planted, and villages sprang up around these culti-
vated fields. The so-called Agricultural Revolution
began, and the way of life of Dar and his people
disappeared along with the dagger-tooth cat.